Dedication

Body in Bog Bay is dedicated to my husband, Bill. Who else could get me to lay on a muddy oyster grant on a freezing December day? Who else would have the patience to calm me down in the face of technical glitches? Who else would dare to remind me that I had better spend more time writing? Who else would happily promote my books? Thanks. Bill. It has been a great run. Bring on more years!

Acknowledgements

A huge debt of gratitude is owed to Dwight Estey. We developed a trusting partnership as he carefully edited drafts of *Body in Bog Bay*. His work vastly improved the book. I also am grateful to family and friends who read my first mystery *Murder at Thoreau Pond* and encouraged me to write a second one. Just asking me if I was writing gave me the incentive to do so. Thanks also to Ethan Estey for the use of his shellfish grant for the cover photo, to my husband Bill for his expertise in self-publishing, and as always thanks to "Oyster Town" for being the unique place it is.

Body

in

Bog Bay

A Cape Cod Mystery

Alice Iacuessa

Old Wharf Press

*Dear Mary Anne + Tony,
Enjoy my Cape Cod mystery.
Thank you for the on going encouragement for my writing endeavors!
Alice*

Published by Old Wharf Press

Copyright © Alice Iacuessa   2013

Published in the United States in 2013 by Old Wharf Press

This mystery is entirely a work of fiction. Names, characters, businesses, organizations, places, events, and incidents either are the product of the author's imagination or are used fictitiously. Any resemblance to actual persons, living or dead, events, or locales is entirely coincidental.

All rights reserved, no parts of this book may be reproduced by any means, graphic electronic, or mechanical, including photocopying, recording, taping, or by any information storage retrieval systems without the written permission of the author or publisher except in the case of brief quotations embodied in critical articles or reviews.

Copies of this book may be purchased at select on-line sellers, select bookstores, or for a signed copy, by email request to old.wharf.press@gmail.com

Cover design and photo: Bill Iacuessa

ISBN-10: 1482039303
ISBN-13: 978-1482039306

Third Edition
August 2013

Chapter 1

"There is nothing like a late June morning on the Heath," said Hannah Brewster as she and her husband, Martin, enjoyed breakfast on the outside terrace of the Kenwood House on Hampstead Heath in north London.

"Yes," Martin replied. "When the weather is nice it is a perfect time to be in London. It is never too hot, and the sun rises at 4 am and doesn't set until after 10pm. Long, lazy days."

"After last weekend's concert on the lawn here at Kenwood we had to wait about a half hour before it was dark enough for fireworks to begin. The evening was beautiful and we had plenty of champagne to share with our friends."

The concerts were as much an excuse to consume a sumptuous picnic than listen to classical music. Concertgoers indulged in delicacies like pate, fine cheeses, the first of the season strawberries, accompanied by champagne.

"We are so lucky to live close by," Hannah said. "We've probably walked or run over most of the eight hundred acres that make up the Heath."

"My favorite run goes through the woods, then through heathland and over the top of Parliament Hill. I usually stop there briefly for its view over the city," Martin replied.

Hannah thought about the Heath. It was a popular place for Londoners to walk, jog, swim or just relax. "We love London and the Heath," Hannah replied. "But it is June again and time to return to Oyster Town for the summer. It is always hard to leave London." Pausing she added, "And when the fall comes it is hard to leave Oyster Town and return here."

"Remember the reaction our families had when we bought land in Oyster Town?" Hannah mused.

Martin thought about Hannah's comment. Hindsight had proved the Brewsters correct in their decision. They were fortunate to have purchased land in Oyster Town on Cape Cod many years ago. At the time they had just started their careers. Their son, Jeff, was a baby. They owned nothing in the States, and they were leaving the country for what they thought would be a one year European experience.

Yes, their families questioned their judgment. In the end, though, they stayed in Europe enjoying their work, she as a teacher in an international school, and he as a consultant. The house in Oyster Town became their summer retreat.

Nearly every time the Brewsters had breakfast at the Kenwood House they stopped to see the small but remarkable art collection housed in the lovely neoclassical building. The architect Robert Adam remodeled the former brick structure between 1764 and 1779 and transformed it into a beautiful villa. Hannah and Martin visited their favorite pieces, a Rembrandt self-portrait, Vermeer's the *Guitar Player* and two pastoral scenes by Boucher.

As they were walking across the Heath back to their apartment, Hannah said that she wanted to do one last thing before leaving London for Cape Cod.

"I want to take a swim this afternoon in the Highgate Ladies Bathing Pond," Hannah told Martin. "The weather has been so warm all June the water should be a comfortable temperature. Do you want to swim in the Men's Pond? Or we could both go to the Mixed Pond."

Martin had some phone calls to make so he begged off. Within the hour Hannah found herself back on the Heath.

Every time she walked down the shady dirt path to the Ladies Bathing Pond she thought of a book a friend had given her called *The Purple Runner*. In it a mysterious but very talented runner piques the curiosity of Heath goers. What always intrigued her was that in the novel, the Purple Runner lived in a hidden, abandoned London underground station. Hannah knew that abandoned stations existed and wondered if there could have been one in this section of the Heath.

She pushed open the iron gate leading to the pond and entered the dressing room. She slipped into her bathing suit, walked out on the dock and slid into the pond. When she first heard of a women's pond, a men's pond, and a mixed bathing pond, she thought the idea old-fashioned, even illegal. However, once she discovered the joy of swimming and relaxing in an environment of all women she came to understand why the public fought when anyone suggested a change to the status quo.

Chapter 2

The Brewsters were packed and ready when the mini-cab came to collect them and take them to Heathrow Airport. They were quiet during the ride. Each lost in thought, musing about this transition they made from one home to the other each year.

After checking their baggage they went through security removing jewelry, shoes, belts.

"No glamour in traveling by air anymore," commented Martin as he rearranged his carry-on after it had been examined by one of the security guards.

"I want to get a book to read on the plane," Hannah said as they passed a book store. "Actually this terminal has so many nice shops, I could spend a lot of time browsing."

In the bookstore she picked up a mystery that looked interesting. She read the reviews: 'Recent and welcome addition to crime fiction'; 'Prolific writer - three books in two years'; 'Intriguing characters and settings'. Hannah paid for the paperback and put it in her purse.

In a short time they were boarded, in their seats and in the air.

Martin flipped through the channels on the plane's entertainment system and finally settled on a movie. Hannah dug out her new mystery and before starting it went to the back flap to read about the author. She examined his picture. It showed a man in his 40s with boyish good looks. He appeared professorial in a dark turtleneck and tweed sport coat. She studied the face carefully. She thought his face revealed a slight smugness, a superiority. But that could just be the pose.

She started to read about the author. Surprised, she nudged Martin. "Look Martin," she said. "The book I bought is written by a man who has a summer house on the Cape. He's a professor and recently has had three very successful mysteries."

She settled herself for what proved to be a very enjoyable read.

They arrived at Boston's Logan Airport. After collecting their luggage, Hannah began to walk toward the bus stop for the Cape, when Martin stopped her.

"I have a surprise for you," he announced. "We are going to the Cape a different way this year. Since we are getting to the Cape nearly three weeks later than usual, I thought we deserved a treat. We are taking the fast ferry to Provincetown."

They took the water taxi from the airport to World Trade Center where they boarded the ferry, a large comfortable catamaran that would bring them to Provincetown in 90 minutes.

"Jeff knows we are coming by ferry and will be there to pick us up," Martin said.

"Well this will be much quicker than the bus which usually takes two hours and then we still have to drive from Hyannis to Oyster Town. Oh! I just remembered it is Saturday. The traffic trying to get over the bridge onto the Cape is a nightmare on Saturdays!"

"I considered booking the traditional ferry which takes three hours but decided that we both would want to get home as quickly as possible," Martin said. "But it might have been fun. I've been told that it can be a real party with sunbathing, drinks and impromptu dancing. Maybe next time."

It was a beautiful, early evening as they crossed Cape Cod Bay to Provincetown Harbor. The summer season had started and the marina was filled with boats. Pleasure boats moored alongside whale watching boats and working fishing boats. It was a colorful, bustling harbor and from the water the town was picturesque with its shops, inns, and houses pressed close to one another. There was a crowd at the pier. Some were there to greet passengers and others just to watch the hustle and bustle as people disembarked.

Jeff looked amused as he waited for his parents to descend the gangplank.

"This is a much better way to arrive on the Cape than by bus. And it's a much shorter drive for me than going to Hyannis," he said giving them a hug. "But why didn't you take the regular ferry? That can be lots of fun."

When Jeff was just out of college and living in Boston, the ferry was his usual way of getting to the Cape and his parents. He always had stories of passengers meeting on the ferry or passengers leaving the ferry and scouting the crowd for a possible partner for the weekend.

"From the stories you used to tell us," Hannah replied, "I think we would be out of place on the party boat. Anyway it was a very nice trip, and it is good to finally be here."

They all piled into Jeff's dilapidated truck and headed to Oyster Town. In less than 25 minutes they were driving down the dirt road to their home on Bog Bay.

"You'll be happy to know that I think I can afford to stay in my house this summer," Jeff said as they approached the Brewster's home which sat on the edge of a marsh.

The previous year Jeff had unexpectedly inherited a small house from an elderly woman he had befriended, but insurance costs and pending winter heating bills meant he had had to rent it for part of the summer and live with his parents. Summer rent was a lucrative way for many home owners in the town to meet their bills. However, this meant that they stayed with family or friends or even at one of the local campgrounds.

"This year I think I budgeted properly and won't need the rental income," he explained.

"But it is expensive owning a house," he complained. "I thought I was really lucky when Lydia left the house to me in her will, but I had a lot more money when I lived with you. And since you are gone most of the year I really had the house to myself."

While Jeff was being nostalgic for the good old days, his father was thinking how nice it was to have the house to themselves. Food didn't constantly disappear from the fridge. He didn't have to listen to Jeff's music. He didn't have to look at Jeff's old truck in the driveway.

After getting his parents' baggage into the house Jeff joked, "Since I haven't seen you for a while I'll come by tomorrow for breakfast. The new bistro carries some great croissants, Dad. You can pick some up in the morning or you can take me out. It'll be your thanks for picking you up in P-town."

Martin rolled his eyes and then laughed. "We'll be jetlagged and up early so what about meeting at 7 at the Sand Bar."

Chapter 3

As the Brewsters arrived at the Sand Bar the next morning they met their neighbor, Ben, who was just leaving.

"Working on your grant this morning?" Martin asked, greeting him.

"It was an early morning low tide so I couldn't do any work, but I wanted to check things out," was his response as they shook hands meeting each other for the first time this summer.

Oyster Town was known for its aquaculture business, especially the growing of oysters. Shellfishermen, like Ben, who held grants on the flats tended to their crop nearly every low tide. When the tide was high the flats were covered with water and it was time for boaters to use the bay.

"How was your winter in London?" he asked.

They talked a bit catching up on each other's activities.

"By the way did you notice that *Windswept* wasn't in your yard?" *Windswept* was the Brewsters' Rhodes 19 sailboat.

Martin looked sheepish. "We got home in the evening yesterday and this morning I never gave the boat a thought. I'm sure I would have gotten to it right after breakfast, though."

"Well you can relax after breakfast or go sailing. I helped Jeff launch your boat last week. He waxed it like you always do and polished the teak."

Hannah laughed, "That's a surprise."

"It sure is!" Martin seconded.

"I think he had some friends visiting and he wanted to take them sailing. He also raced in last Sunday's regatta and did quite well, a first and a third if I recall," Ben said as he walked to his truck waving good-bye.

Jeff was in the Sand Bar with Miyu Lee, a young pretty Asian woman who served as the town's chief of police. It was unusual to have someone so young and a female serve in that position but she was smart and competent and the town was proud of its decision to break from the mold of middle aged male chiefs.

"Hi Mr. and Mrs. B," Miyu called to the Brewsters. "Jeff told me you were returning from London, and I wanted to say hi before I started work this morning."

She continued, "I also wanted to explain to you in person about the ticket."

"What ticket?" Hannah asked trying to remember if she and Martin had received any tickets recently.

Miyu was a bit tentative but then became direct. "If you recall last year when we were working on that blackmail-murder case, I saw proof that you were pulling a boat trailer with an expired license plate."

Martin nodded in agreement.

"Well you can imagine my predicament last week when I saw Jeff pulling your boat with the same unlicensed trailer on the state highway. He was on his way to launch the boat at the marina."

Jeff laughed, "Mom and Dad, you know that Miyu is an honest cop, right."

They both agreed.

"Well she pulled me over and gave me a ticket."

"Like father, like son?" Chief Lee queried.

Martin looked pained. "How much was the ticket?"

"I am sure you can afford it. And," she emphasized, "afford to insure your boat trailer each year."

"I always liked getting away with pulling the unlicensed trailer," Martin complained after Miyu left. "We only use it twice a summer, once to launch the boat and the other to take it out of the water, probably a total of 5 miles. I feel I'm losing a bit of my summer ritual."

Hannah changed the subject and they talked about Jeff's racing success the previous Sunday.

"Oh, talking about boats reminds me," Jeff said. "When we were launching *Windswept* a man came over and asked questions about the boat. He said he had just moved to Oyster Town and was interested in buying a sailboat, maybe a Rhodes. I told him you would be happy to talk with him when you got back from London. He gave me his card." Jeff passed the card to Martin.

Hannah looked at it and said, "That name seems familiar."

"I'll give him a call in a few days and maybe we can take him for a sail and get him familiar with the Rhodes," Martin said. Then he added, "Thanks, Jeff, for getting the boat ready and launched."

Jeff glanced at his watch and said he had a meeting in Provincetown with his editor, Dixie Groznik. Jeff wrote for the local paper, *The Cape Chronicle* and supplemented his income with freelance projects and in the summer playing guitar twice weekly at the Sand Bar.

As he was about to leave a young blond woman walked in catching the attention of a number of the patrons who were also having an early breakfast. She was dressed in skin tight jeans with a tight t-shirt decorated with sparkling beads. Her hair was done up in two pigtails with large red ribbons.

"Oh you are back!" she purred, coming over to the Brewsters, saying to Martin, "What about a big smooch?"

Under Hannah's watchful eye he gave her a chaste kiss on the cheek and said, "Hello Lola. It is good to be back in Oyster Town."

She agreed telling them that she also had just gotten back. "I was in New York City for the winter. Gabe and Ollie helped me get a part in an off-Broadway production that ran several months. Did you know that Gabe and Ollie have lots of contacts in New York? Even though Oyster Town's Bay Players Theater is just a small local summer theater it has an excellent reputation. When New York directors heard that I worked here for Gabe and Ollie it really opened doors."

She tossed her pigtails and glanced around the room blowing a kiss to one of the local shellfishermen who was ogling her. She turned back to the Brewsters and said, "Now I am back and ready to be a star here again this summer."

She draped her arm over Jeff's shoulder. "Plus I am so happy to be Jeff's neighbor again. I really missed him. A girl needs a strong handsome man around." She winked at Jeff and Martin.

"Am I invisible?" Hannah asked as Lola sauntered to the bar to order a coffee.

"Well you don't fit the category of strong handsome man," Martin said grinning and puffing out his chest giving a he-man gesture.

Chapter 4

It was a beautiful morning for a run, sunny and dry, even a little cool for the start of July. "Do you want to run together this morning?" Martin asked as Hannah did some pre-run stretching

"If you don't mind going at my slower pace," she responded. "I was planning on running to Marconi Site in the National Seashore and then down Wireless Road, Le Count Hollow Road, and home via the bike trail. What do you think?"

"Fine by me," Martin answered. "That should be about 4 miles."

The Cape Cod National Seashore was created in 1961 when President John Kennedy signed a bill into law that set aside 44,000 acres including 40 miles of undeveloped beach along the Atlantic Ocean. The main purpose was to preserve the pristine coast but by chance other important elements were included in the park such as the site where in 1903 Guglielmo Marconi sent the first transatlantic wireless message which was from President Theodore Roosevelt to King Edward VII of England.

During their run the Brewsters reached the site of that historic transmission. It stood on the edge of a 90 foot cliff overlooking the Atlantic Ocean. "Not much left of the 210 foot transmitting towers," Hannah mused. "At low tide we've seen the remaining bases of two towers out there in the ocean."

"Erosion has taken its toll," mused Martin. They say these cliffs erode three feet a year, but some years the erosion is much greater. The whole site is now threatened."

They left the paved road and entered the woods running down Wireless Road, a sandy path that also served as part of the Atlantic White Cedar Swamp Trail, one of the self-guided trails in the National Seashore.

"This is the road that horses and carts used to supply Marconi and his workers," Martin said.

"And the path Charlie Paine took when he announced the successful transatlantic wireless message. Marconi told him to ride like the wind and Charlie did so until he was out of Marconi's sight. Then he slowed down and in typical old Cape Cod fashion, decided he wasn't going to exhaust his horse for anyone, not even Marconi. The announcement to the world of this success could wait a little longer."

"That independent streak is still part of the nature of Cape Codders," Martin said. "And maybe especially those from Oyster Town."

When they arrived home there was a message on the phone for Hannah from Izzy Smith, President of the Board of Directors for the local historical museum, the Captain Kendrick House. Hannah was a volunteer at the museum and was expecting Izzy to phone to discuss the times he needed her this summer.

She returned his call and after a few pleasantries Hannah said, "I am looking forward to working at the museum again. Do you want me to come on Monday mornings?" This was the time she had worked the past two years.

"Actually Hannah I have some ideas I want to share with you. Can you meet me for lunch at the Pirates Pub?"

They agreed to meet at one.

At the start of the summer the Brewsters had promised themselves that they would try to sail every chance they got and schedule other things around sailing.

"High tide today is at 10 so it is too late to go sailing," said Martin when she told him about her lunch engagement.

The Brewsters moored their sailboat down the road in Bog Bay. That and nearby Grampus Creek were tidal. When the tide went out oyster grants emerged along with oystermen and their trucks. When the tide came in they could start sailing. They could sail three hours before high tide and had to be back at their mooring three hours after high tide. Beyond Bog Bay and Grampus Creek was Billingsgate Bay and Cape Cod Bay. These were navigable at all times and sometimes Hannah and Martin would go for an all-day sail in these waters going out on an ebb tide and returning to their mooring on the rising tide.

Hannah drove into town in the MG with the top down enjoying the breeze and sun on her face. Their practical car was a Volvo station wagon. Their fun car was the old model MG Martin had bought and shipped from Britain a few years ago.

The Pirate's Pub was across the street from the Captain Kendrick House, and Hannah frequently stopped there for a coffee before or after volunteering at the local museum. She parked behind town hall and waved to Izzy who was sitting at a table on the outside patio.

Often several local shellfishermen patronized the pub, but the tide was going out. They were about to go to work on the flats. So at the moment the pub was mainly filled with tourists.

Izzy and Hannah both ordered oyster bisque and while waiting for their lunch Izzy explained the purpose of their meeting.

"Hannah, I know you enjoy working at the museum, meeting people and answering their questions but I was hoping this summer you would take on a special project," Izzy began.

Hannah encouraged him to continue.

"The museum applied for and received a cultural grant for a new exhibit. Heaven knows we need one since we haven't made any changes to the museum in decades."

"That is true but people like the local flavor of the museum and don't even complain about the lack of air conditioning on hot, humid days."

"We don't intend to change the character of the museum," Izzy quickly added. "We just plan to create an exhibit on an important aspect of the town that we should be featuring more prominently."

"So what is the subject of this new exhibit?" Hannah asked, hoping it would be something that interested her since she knew she would not refuse Izzy's request.

"You know, of course, that in the early 1800s Billingsgate Island was home to a small but successful fishing community."

"Yes," said Hannah. "I know a bit of the history. By the early 1900s the settlement was abandoned since the island was being eroded by the sea. Martin and I have sailed to Billingsgate and at low tide it is like a large sand bar. You can still see evidence of the rip rap that was bought in to protect the island from flooding." Hannah began to warm to the subject. "It didn't help, though," she added.

"Before the island was completely eroded several of the buildings were floated to shore and became part of Oyster Town. That is what the subject of the new exhibit will be – the buildings in town that used to be located on Billingsgate," Izzy announced.

"I would like you to do the research on these buildings and probably take photos. I heard Martin is an excellent photographer, maybe he could help, or Jeff."

Hannah enjoyed volunteering one morning a week at the museum. She felt it anchored her week, but this project appealed to her. She could do research at both the library and the museum and then visit the buildings. She would enjoy being out and about in the town.

She enthusiastically agreed to the project and asked, "When do you want my research completed?"

"I asked Abby Wiley if she would design the display at the museum which requires some carpentry as well as layout of materials. I can pay her with some of the grant money and like many of the local artists she can use it. Abby works as a waitress during the summer so she can't start working on the display until after Labor Day. Also creating this will result in part of the museum being disrupted. We close after Labor Day so that works well for her and us."

"That works well for me also since it gives me about eight weeks to do my research and photos. I will be in Oyster Town until the beginning of October so I will be around if Abby needs me once she starts to install the exhibit."

They discussed the logistics of the project further, and Hannah's enthusiasm grew. She was eager to tell Martin about it.

As she left the pub there was a commotion in the street. A woman with a long multi-colored dress, a turban to match and large, round earrings was riding her horse down Main Street gesturing to the cars and pedestrians. As she approached the pub she dismounted and began to direct traffic.

"Okay, lady, you can cross now," she hollered to Hannah who was standing near the crosswalk.

Drivers started beeping their horns, and the woman ignored them blocking the road with her horse. Her mouth was full of gum but she took a fresh piece as she gestured to the traffic surrounding her.

"All right Maddie get a move on," a commanding voice ordered. Hannah turned and saw Gino Santos one of Oyster Town's policemen approach the woman.

At the same moment Chief Lee arrived in a patrol car. "The station got a report of a disturbance on Route 6. Some woman on a horse directing traffic. It looks as if she moved here to Main Street," she said joining Santos.

Maddie put her hands on her hips, challenging the police officers.

"Let me deal with this," Santos said to the chief. "I know Madeleine. She used to live in town years ago. She trusts me since I am a local."

Sometimes Chief Lee bristled when Santos or other police officers reminded her that she was an outsider. She had come to understand the status of those living on the Cape. There were the locals, born and raised on the Cape; the wash-a-shores who may have lived most of their lives on the Cape but who would never be locals. Then were people like herself who had recently settled on the Cape and finally the summer people and tourists.

This time, however, Chief Lee acknowledged that it might be best to let Santos handle the situation. She felt that in this particular case he probably had a better understanding of how to handle the woman.

Santos swaggered over to Maddie and said, "Madeleine, you're causing a public disturbance. I can arrest you for that."

Maddie laughed saying, "Gino, don't be a dumb fool. You aren't arresting anyone. You know that Maddie can jinx you. But since we are old friends, I'll be a good girl. I'll just tie up my horse and sit here on the park bench. That's legal isn't it?"

Santos stepped aside to let her move to the bench on the town green in front of town hall. He then tried to deal with the commotion. There were people crowded on the sidewalk watching the interaction. Many had left their cars in the road, and Santos was trying to get them to go back to their vehicles so he could restore the normal flow of traffic.

Maddie shouted advice to him, laughing as he became more and more frustrated. "You should have let me direct the traffic. I'm a pro."

Hannah was standing near the town green waiting for the traffic to clear so she could drive home. Maddie gestured to her. "Come over here. I have something to tell you."

Hannah hesitated but the woman kept calling her.

When she got close enough Maddie grabbed her hand and said mysteriously, "If you cross my palm with silver I can tell your fortune. I have the gift."

Hannah tried to decline politely, but Maddie laughed and dug into her pocket. She pulled out some more gum and a card with her name encircled with celestial bodies. "I predict you will want information from me in the future. Don't lose my card."

"Well that was strange!" Hannah said to herself as she drove home. Later, telling Martin about the encounter she said, "I do recollect someone talking about a woman like Maddie living in Oyster Town a number of years ago. We'll have to ask Miyu about this."

Chapter 5

"It doesn't look like the winds will be good for sailing," Martin said as he entered the house after collecting the newspaper which as usual had been left in the dirt driveway. "Let's have breakfast at the new bistro. Then we can go to Jeff's and swim in the pond."

It was a warm, still, summer morning as they sat on the porch of the bistro enjoying coffee and croissants. "These croissants are delicious," Hannah said as the buttery pastry crumbled on her plate. "They are so good we could be in Paris."

A man at a table near them nodded to them. "Did you know that the owners shipped the bread and pastry ovens from Europe? It tastes as if they even order the butter and flour from France."

"Oyster Town gets better and better," said Hannah. "Authentic croissants accompanied by coffee from locally roasted beans."

"Speaking of local things," Martin responded, "let's go to the beach sticker shack and get our clamming licenses. We never got them last year and I missed getting our own clams and oysters."

Arriving at the harbor parking lot they joined a small line that had formed to buy beach stickers and shellfish licenses. The Brewsters, who had already purchased their beach stickers, were there to obtain shellfish permits and with these in hand they left the shack to find the marina becoming a chaotic mass of cars and pedestrians. Maddie had arrived on her horse.

She was blocking the road and rerouting traffic through the marina parking lot.

"Let's get out of here while we can," Hannah said as they got into their MG. "I know that this can turn into a huge mess."

Martin nodded saying, "Time for a swim." They turned onto a narrow dirt road at the Bayberry Inn. The road ended at a small traditional half Cape house built in the 1880's. Jeff was sitting on his deck with his laptop on a small table and empty cups of coffee surrounding him.

Hannah and Martin knew this was not the time to talk to him since he was in the middle of writing a story for the paper. They turned their attention to the beautifully clear pond only steps away from Jeff's deck.

"Well, well, well!" Hannah murmured as she saw a bikini top draped over the deck railing.

"Looks like Lola also decided to take a swim," Martin said as he waved to the young woman in the water.

"Yes and if I am right she forgot to put on the top to her bathing suit," Hannah said wryly and she pointed to the bikini top. "What should we do?"

Martin grinned and sat in a deck chair. "I think I'll just take in the view."

"Martin!" Hannah said in exasperation.

"Honey, you know I'm kidding. I am a gentleman. Plus I might have a heart attack when she comes out of the water. I'll go inside. Might take a peek through the window though!"

He had just turned to go in the house when Lola called to Hannah to bring her a towel.

"Well, she has some self-respect after all," Hannah muttered to Martin.

After the Brewsters finished their swim, they joined Lola and Jeff.

Jeff had exchanged his lap top for one of his guitars but stopped strumming to tell his mother that Brocton Phillip's gallery may have been one of the floaters, buildings that had been moved from Billingsgate Island, that she was researching for the museum.

"Lydia's shop might be one too," said Lola.

Lola was living in an apartment above what had been Lydia's Antique Emporium. "Do you remember the unfortunate situation with the maps from the Kendrick House last year?" she asked.

"How could they forget," thought Hannah, "since the maps were involved in a murder investigation."

"One was an old map of this area. When I studied the map it seemed to me that Brocton's building and Lydia's were attached."

This piqued Hannah's interest and she made note to look for those maps at the museum.

Lola finished by making a plea, "When you are looking at old maps see if you can find anything about who rightfully owns Lydia's building."

In her will Lydia left Jeff her small house. Just up the road a larger building with the antique shop and apartment above was bequeathed to her niece, Veronica.

"My friend Veronica is happy to let me live in the apartment. She has tons of money and is living in Europe so at the moment doesn't need the place," Lola said. "I decided to rent out the old antique shop so I could contribute to the taxes and upkeep. I am renting it as a gallery space to Armand DeCristo. But Brocton is starting to pester me again about its rightful ownership."

"You know all winter when I was in New York City I didn't hear a word from him. But since I've been back he's been bringing up his old claim to the property. He says Lydia never owned it and that it belongs to him."

"I think he just wants me to leave. Yesterday he told me that he suspects my septic system is failing and polluting the pond. Veronica won't want the hassle of getting all the permits required to update the system so I would have to move. Probably leave Oyster Town." She gave a pout and cuddled up to Jeff. "Poor me just as I've gotten a start on my career. What will happen to me?"

"What will happen to the pond if you are polluting it?" Hannah responded.

"I don't believe the septic system is failing," Lola responded. "I think Brocton is just mad at me and at Armand. Last month Armand told Brocton he would not show his paintings in Brocton's gallery anymore."

"You and dad missed this," Jeff said jumping in. "Brocton decided to introduce two new artists in his gallery. Armand thought their work 'insignificant', at least compared to his. When Dixie wrote a negative review in *The Cape Chronicle* about the quality of one of the artists, Armand was determined not have his work in the same gallery."

"So Armand was looking for a new space to display and I was looking for a tenant. It was perfect. Except that Brocton started in again about ownership."

"Seems strange to me," Martin said joining the conversation. "Why would Brocton want the property if the septic is failing? He would have a huge expense to get things updated. When property is so close to water like this pond, regulations are strict."

Hannah heard a car approaching the house. A few moments later Miyu joined them on the deck. She gave an amused look as she glanced at Lola sitting on the floor with her back against Jeff's knees.

"I just saw Dixie," Miyu said addressing Jeff. "Your cell phone is off and she has been trying to call you about an assignment."

Jeff jumped up and left the gathering to call his editor.

Lola said her good byes and swinging her hips, strolled up the road to her apartment.

Hannah decided to take this opportunity to ask Miyu about Maddie.

Miyu told her what she knew of the woman. "From what I have learned about her, she is very eccentric, which is why some of the locals call her Mad Maddie. She lived in Oyster Town a while ago. She left about 10 or 12 years ago. I don't know why she returned, but she does own property here. I've been told it is a simple cabin with a small barn for her horse."

"What does she do for money? She has taxes to pay and she must feed herself and her horse?"

"I don't know," was Miyu's reply. "I know she tells fortunes and makes predictions and casts spells, good and bad. How many clients she has, though, I don't know. But fishermen and boaters, in general, can be a superstitious lot."

Chapter 6

On Wednesday morning Martin was off to the transfer station with their trash and recyclables, and Hannah to Town Hall and the Captain Kendrick House to search for information on floaters.

When they met up for lunch Hannah excitedly waved the notes she had taken during her research. Sitting on the deck overlooking the marsh Hannah said, "You know I like the marsh at low tide almost as much as I do when the tide is in. In the spring and summer the marsh grasses are such a lovely bright green and in the fall it changes to yellow, russet, and brown."

"And the few winters we have been here it can be frosty with a cold wind blowing across it. Good thing our house is well insulated! The old timers wouldn't have chosen this spot for a house. They didn't care about a view. When they returned from the sea many did not want to look out at it since it reminded them of the dangers they faced. They built in the hollows where they were protected from the weather."

"True," Hannah said then pointed to her notes. "But a number of them did settle on Billingsgate Island which offered little protection from the elements. I learned that in its heyday Billingsgate had over thirty houses and its own school. It even had a lighthouse that was built in 1822."

"That is earlier than the lighthouse at Mayo Beach," Martin replied. "That one was established in 1838."

"Right I remember the articles about it a few years ago when it was found in California."

"It was a surprising piece of news for most people in Oyster Town," said Martin. "The Mayo Beach lighthouse was discontinued in 1922 and no one knew what happened to it. Most thought it was demolished for scrap. Recently, it was located near San Francisco. It's part of a youth hostel."

"Well no Billingsgate Light exists. As a matter of fact 12 years after it was built, the first one was undermined by the sea and had to be replaced. The island continued to erode rapidly and the second lighthouse, even though it was on higher ground, had sand and water washing through it during storms. The inhabitants tried to save their homes, buildings, and the island itself by putting a thousand feet of jetties and bulkheads around the island. We see remains of these when we sail out there."

"Just like today. Lots of people with homes on the water are building sea walls and rock revetments hoping to stop erosion," Martin commented.

"Maybe they will be luckier," Hannah said. "But by 1915 the only occupants of Billingsgate were the lighthouse keeper and his family. And on December 26 of that year erosion took its toll on the lighthouse and it toppled in a storm."

"When can we do a sail to Billingsgate? I'd like you to take some photos of what remains today for the museum's exhibit."

Martin went into his study to get a tide chart. "We want to be on the island at low tide when it is visible and we can walk around. Maybe even do some clamming. Early next week would work."

"If the weather is good, let's plan on going Monday. We can bring beach chairs, an umbrella, lunch," Hannah said enthusiastically.

Martin continued studying the tide chart. "Monday it is!" he said as he carried his lunch dishes into the kitchen. "Right now I have some banking business to take care of."

"And I want to write up the notes I took this morning," she replied taking her laptop out of its case. "I plan to work until 5:30 and then get ready for the benefit cocktail party."

The evening was warm with the sun still high in the sky. Martin drove the MG across the small wooden bridge leading to Lieutenant Island. Turning onto a dirt road and seeing cars parked all along the narrow road, Hannah said, "It seems as if everyone is here already."

The benefit, a yearly event in their summer calendar, was being hosted by Doc and his wife, Elena, who greeted them at the door of their contemporary home.

"You've been back nearly a week and this is the first time we've seen one another," said Elena.

"Yes, we were late getting to the Cape this summer. Jeff put *Windswept* in the water so we missed the tradition of all of us getting together to launch our boats," Martin said giving her a welcoming kiss on the cheek.

Doc was one of a handful of friends who raced their Rhodes 19s most weekends. He welcomed the Brewsters back to Oyster Town. "You know Jeff did very well in the races last week. He read the wind and currents, taking tacks that the rest of us should have taken."

Martin and Doc continued talking about sailing as they headed to the big deck where the bar was set up. "Gerard and Ted are here tonight," Doc said, motioning to two men standing by the bar. "They both plan on racing again this summer."

Hannah followed with Elena. "It was very good of you to host the benefit this year," Hannah said knowing the preparation it took. "But you always make things look so easy - the perfect hostess."

"You know that Doc and I love The Bay Players Theater so we are happy to do what we can to support it."

Glasses of wine in hand Martin and Hannah enjoyed the view from the deck looking across Grampus Bay, where they could see their boat moored in Bog Bay.

Some people were sitting in wicker chairs while others were gathered in small groups chatting. The Brewsters recognized Ollie and Gabe who co-founded the theater. They were beaming, pleased with the large turnout.

Ollie waved to Hannah. "Welcome back. Did you see some good theater this winter in London?

Gabe took Hannah's hand and kissed it with a flourish. "Here at the Bay Players Theater we have a very exciting season planned this summer."

Ollie added, "We picked some of the plays especially for Lola. She was such a surprise hit last year."

As he said this they were joined by a large, balding man sporting an apricot ascot. "Well she isn't a hit with me," he said haughtily. "And I won't be attending any of the plays she is in."

"Brocton, you have to understand that she was a big box office draw last year," Gabe said trying to reason with the gallery owner.

They continued discussing this delicate point as Hannah was drawn away from the group by a sinewy man with bleach blond hair, dressed in casual pants, an expensive white linen shirt and wearing designer flip-flops.

"Here comes danger," Hannah said to herself as she was kissed by Armand DeCristo.

"I thought you would never return to the Cape," he said leering at Hannah. "I began to think my summer would be incomplete." He slipped his arm around her waist leading her back to the bar. "I must lure you back to my cozy cottage on the water. I have some new paintings to show you."

Hannah extricated herself from Armand and did not respond to his invitation.

"Damn!" whispered the artist to Hannah. "Competition is coming this way."

Hannah looked across the room to see Martin walking toward her. He was in an animated conversation with a man who looked vaguely familiar.

"Do you mean Martin?" Hannah laughed. "If so, you are right. He definitely is your competition. If you mean the other man," she hesitated, sizing him up. "Many women would find him very attractive. For me, though, he is too good looking, too pretty. I prefer men who look more masculine. Have more character in their faces."

"Then I suit the bill," said Armand turning his head. "Look at this strong manly profile."

"Hannah," Martin said as he approached. "Let me introduce you to Troy Oliver. He is the author of the mystery you bought in London before flying back to the Cape."

"I thought you looked familiar," Hannah said as she acknowledged the introduction. "I enjoyed the book. I bought it at Heathrow for the plane ride to Boston."

Troy explained that his books sold well in England precisely because some of the scenes were set in London.

The conversation returned to sailing and Troy Oliver said, "It would be nice to go for a sail to get the feel of the Rhodes before I buy one. It's been a while since I was on a boat that small. I have been sailing much larger boats, 35 to 50 feet, but everyone says that a Rhodes is ideal for Billingsgate Bay."

"It is perfect for day sailing which is what most of us do. We also race once a week in the summer," Hannah commented.

"Racing? Now there's a challenge. I haven't raced in years. I used to crew in some big regattas when I lived in California."

"Would you like to sail tomorrow?" Martin asked.

They arranged to meet at eleven to sail for a couple of hours, and Hannah said she would fix lobster rolls for their lunch.

On the short drive home Hannah said to Martin, "Well it seems as if our author has done a lot of big time sailing - big boats, big races. I am curious to see how he handles *Windswept* tomorrow."

"So you are joining us on the boat?" Martin asked.

"I wouldn't miss it," was Hannah's answer.

Chapter 7

After finishing breakfast on the deck Martin went to the fish market to buy lobster for the sailing lunch with Troy, and Hannah went to tend her vegetable garden. She didn't have a true green thumb, but every year she managed to grow a sufficient amount of vegetables which encouraged her to continue. She was unsure how well her lettuce would do since she had planted the seeds rather late in the season. The tomatoes, on the other hand, were doing beautifully. Much of the credit at this stage belonged to the 'Oyster Town Tomato Lady' from whom she bought seedlings. This year Stella had raved about 'Bloody Butcher', 'Chadwick Cherry', 'Hillbilly'.

"Hannah," she enthused. "With names like that you have to have these tomatoes in your garden."

Interesting names or not the plants were thriving. Green beans and cucumbers seemed to have a good start and the hot peppers looked as if they might be a successful crop as well. This year Hannah planned to be on the Cape into the fall so hoped to plant some cool weather crops like kale later in the summer.

The sun felt warm and pleasant on her back as she watered and weeded. When Martin returned from the market she heard the crunch of the car tires on the sand driveway. Several minutes later he joined her in the garden. She looked up as he approached and saw he was frowning.

"What's up?" she asked, wondering why he seemed upset.

"I just listened to a message on the phone," Martin explained. "Apparently Troy Oliver called while I was at the market and you were in the garden. He cancelled his sail with us today. Said a friend called and asked him to go on a boating excursion from Falmouth to Edgartown. Something about the friend didn't feel confident enough on his own. He needed Troy along."

"Well that's a bit rude," said Hannah. "He could have told his friend he had a previous engagement."

"Oh well," sighed Martin. "Maybe there is more to the story and Troy will explain when we see him again. However, we now have two lobsters."

"And the day to fill," Hannah remarked. "I have a suggestion. Let's boil the lobsters and make lobster salad for lobster rolls as we had planned. Pack some pickles and fruit and take a bike ride."

Martin looked pensive. "Normally I would want to sail but this business with Troy has ruined the idea for me. Yes. Let's bike. I would like to bike around some of the kettle ponds. We could take a swim in one or two of them and have our picnic along the way."

They changed into clothes appropriate for biking and Martin got two panniers from the basement. "We can put the lunch in these with some ice packs," he said securing them to his bike.

Shortly, the Brewsters were deep in the National Seashore following a route that passed by a number of isolated ponds. As they approached a spot that gave them access to a small beach and swimming, they saw Maddie approaching them riding her horse.

Maddie waved and dismounted. She studied them both intently and shifted the gum in her mouth.

"A lady in town said you wanted information about the buildings that were moved to Oyster Town from Billingsgate," she said addressing Hannah.

Before Hannah could respond, Maddie continued, "I know a lot about those buildings. I even lived in one of the houses."

Hannah wanted to ask which one but Maddie was determined to control the conversation. "I want you to know that part of my power comes from learning people's stories. Everyone has stories."

She added more gum to her already full mouth. "Let me tell you the true story of the disappearance of Billingsgate." She held out her hand and rubbed it with her other hand. A gesture meaning she wanted to be paid.

Hannah felt like they were in the clutches of the Ancient Mariner whose story must be told. Martin sighed and gave Maddie twenty dollars which she quickly shoved in the pocket of her swirling skirt.

When she was sure they were attentive Maddie began, "Billingsgate supported a real fishing village. It had 60 acres, homes, a lighthouse, a school, a store. Now folks say that it all disappeared due to erosion but there is a darker story. A man from the island was accused of a crime for which the punishment was death. All through the trial he swore he was innocent. But he was found guilty and sentenced to be hung. As he approached the gallows he looked at the crowd gathered there to witness his death. Glaring at them he once again claimed he was innocent and predicted that if he were hanged the island would disappear under the sea. He was hung and it disappeared."

Even though it was warm Hannah felt a chill. It wasn't so much the story as the way Maddie told it with her eyes rolled back in her head as if she were in a trance.

Then the spell was broken as Maddie gave a cackling laugh stuffed more gum in her mouth and mounted her horse. As she left she called out, "I know more stories. There are lots of them in town. People who are not what they say they are. People who have secrets. People who have a past. People who have hidden things. One could make a lot of money knowing Oyster Town's secrets."

"That was creepy," said Hannah as they watched Maddie ride out of sight.

"C'mon," said Martin. "Let's go for a swim."

After their swim they sat in the sun and ate lunch before continuing their bike ride. "Maddie didn't really tell us much about the Billingsgate buildings," Martin mused.

"No," Hannah laughed. "I guess it wasn't worth twenty dollars. From my research I've learned a lot more than what she told us. One example is the seafood restaurant near Main Street. Its dining room dates back to 1750 when it was built on Billingsgate as a house for a whaling captain. There is a lot of speculation about others. For example there is some evidence that Lola and Brocton's places were transported from Billingsgate. Also many people feel a number of the buildings in the area near the harbor were also floaters. But, Izzy told me that some of the buildings in that area were brought from Bound Brook Island which was a large early Oyster Town settlement."

Martin nodded and reminded Hannah of the plaque in the woods on Bound Brook Island commemorating an early Oyster Town school house that had stood on that spot.

When the Brewsters returned home there was a message on the phone from Jeff. He said he had four tickets to the new play at the Bay Players Theatre. "It is opening night. Do you want to go? Miyu will be there." Then he added, "Lola is starring."

It was a pleasant evening and people were milling about outside. Shortly before eight the small crowd began to file into the theater.

"I supposed we should go in now if we want four seats together," said Hannah.

Martin concurred, "The theater is so small every seat is a good one, but yes we do want to sit together so let's go in."

The theater, sometimes nicknamed The Box, was just that – a rectangular room with the stage at one side and 12 tiers of seats facing the stage. It sat about a hundred people but its productions were excellent and cutting edge so they were often reviewed in the Boston and New York newspapers. This evening's play was a provocative one act dark comedy which demanded much from the actors, as well as the audience.

After the play the foursome walked to the restaurant across the road where they sat on the deck for after theater drinks.

"Lola never ceases to amaze me," said Miyu. "Tonight she was mesmerizing as a woman scheming and clawing to reach the top. Yet last year she brilliantly played a ditzy housewife addicted to clothes shopping."

At that moment Lola walked in with Gabe and Ollie.

"It looks as if you have another hit," Jeff called out to them.

Lola grinned at him. "So you like demanding, dangerous women," she challenged.

Miyu answered for him, "He liked the way you portrayed the character not necessarily the character."

"Oh that's okay," was Lola's response. "I can play any number of roles," she purred at Jeff. "What kind of woman do you want me to be?"

Jeff ignored the comment and asked what they would like to have to drink. "My dad is paying," he added grinning at his surprised father.

After conversation about the play, Lola brought up the topic of Brocton Phillips. "Brocton certainly is a strange one," she mused. She explained that she was cleaning out the basement of the former antique shop. "As my new tenant, Armand will use the old antique shop space to exhibit and sell his paintings, and I wanted to give him some storage room in the basement."

She went on to say how surprised she was when Brocton offered to help her. "He was very sweet and seems to have forgotten the trouble he has given me about who actually is the rightful owner of the shop and apartment and that crazy business about a faulty septic system." She tossed her long blond hair for effect.

She explained that he said he would go through all the items in the basement and categorize them. Some could go to a friend of his in the antique business who would sell them on consignment. Some could go to the Charity Shop, some to the Swap Shop at the recycling center. "He even offered to sell some things at the weekend flea market! I guess I trust him. This is a big dirty job and he is saving me time and energy. Of course I don't own any of this so I will have to get my friend Veronica's approval. But, that won't be a problem," she added confidently. "She will agree to anything I suggest."

Hannah thought about the trust Veronica, Aunt Lydia's heir, had in Lola but remembered that she was supposedly very wealthy and the shop, its contents, and the apartment above merely a nuisance for her. Her thoughts were interrupted by Martin.

"It is hard to picture Brocton in his silk shirt and ascot cleaning out a basement," he said. "Maybe you should get a second opinion before you let him do any selling or giving away."

"You could consult Izzy," added Hannah. "As president of the museum Board of Directors, he knows a lot about antiques, bric-a-brac and their worth."

Jeff and Miyu finished their drinks and were taking their leave. Lola stopped them and said, "Maybe I'll come down to your house, Jeff, after I leave here. It always takes me a bit of time to unwind after a performance."

Miyu looked meaningfully at Jeff. "Not tonight Lola," he said. "Miyu and I want to enjoy the moonlight on the pond alone."

Lola shrugged her shoulders and said, "No problem. I think I'll go over to Armand's. He and I can enjoy the moonlight on the bay together."

Chapter 8

After a short morning run along the beach, Hannah jumped in the MG and headed to the farmers' market in Orleans. She admired the various produce and wished that she could grow more than she did in her little garden.

She gathered her purchases and walked back to her car. As she did so she passed the Ocean Wave Bookstore and noticed a sign announcing that Troy Oliver was signing copies of his new book that morning. Hannah was still a bit miffed about Troy's last minute phone call announcing he was not going to sail with them. She wondered what he would say when she bought his latest book and asked him to sign it.

The store was busy and there was a line of mainly women waiting for Troy's signature. The line moved slowly since Troy chatted with each woman, giving them a big smile, winking at them, using his boyish good looks to his advantage.

When Hannah approached the table he looked up with the practiced smile already in place. Recognizing who it was, however, Troy got up from the chair to give her a kiss on the cheek. Hannah was aware of the looks she was given by some of the other women in the shop and also realized that she was allowing herself to be charmed by Troy.

"Hannah," he said. "I was planning on phoning you and Martin today. I owe you an explanation about why I cancelled my sail with you yesterday. It must have seemed a bit abrupt since I did so at the last minute, but let me explain." He seemed genuinely concerned but also glanced at the line of people waiting for his signature.

"How long do you expect to be here at the bookstore?" Hannah asked. "I have to go to the hardware store. It'll take me about a half hour."

"Perfect," Troy answered giving her an especially big smile, showing his perfect, white teeth. "I will meet you at the café next door. We can have lunch."

They both ordered the sandwich special and Troy began his explanation. "I was really looking forward to sailing with you and testing the Rhodes 19 since I was very serious about buying one. But an old friend called me rather late the night before our planned sail. He told me he was scheduled for hip surgery next week and would be recuperating most of the summer. He wanted to have one last boating trip this summer before his operation and asked if I would go with him from Falmouth to Edgartown. He didn't feel that he could make the trip on his own. So I said of course I would go. I knew you and Martin would understand." He gave her a sincere look of apology.

Hannah smiled and said something about scheduling another time for the sail.

"That would be nice," Troy replied. "But I changed my mind about buying a Rhodes. You see my friend told me that I could use his boat this summer. He said he would enjoy thinking of me on the water."

"He must be a good friend," Hannah said. "What kind of boat does he have?"

Troy looked at her warily. "Are you a sailing purist? If so you might not like the fact that it is a Grady White power boat."

Hannah laughed. "No I am not a purist. I enjoy being on the water whether it is a power boat or a sail boat."

"Well then we can set a time for the three of us to motor up to P-town."

They were interrupted by a middle aged woman who clearly was enamored of Troy. She apologized for intruding but explained she had bought his book after he left the store. "I am sorry to bother you, but I admire your books and want to give a signed copy to my sister for her birthday. Do you mind?"

Troy gave his famous smile and the woman nearly melted.

"I don't know how you do it," she said. "You are a prolific writer. Isn't this your third book in less than three years."

"I've been very lucky so far. The inspiration for the books has come very easily. Plus I told my university that I only wanted to teach one course in the spring semester which gave me time to write."

The woman said she was going to London in the fall and wanted to go to some of the places he described in his books.

When she left Hannah started to talk about London and some of her favorite places but Troy seemed impatient to get away. "I am sorry Hannah. I'd love to talk about one of my favorite cities but I must go. I am writing another book and I must keep myself on a schedule."

That reminded Hannah that she too had things to do. She had a meeting with Izzy to discuss the progress she was making on her project for the Captain Kendrick House.

As she approached the museum she saw on the

steps a ceramic pineapple, a symbol of welcome in the old seafaring communities. Every morning a volunteer put it out to announce that the museum was open for the day. Izzy greeted her and they squeezed into the tiny office room at the back of the museum.

"We really could use more space for the office and a break room for volunteers," Izzy said as he pulled out a chair for Hannah. "But this building is an historic one and we can't do any alterations to it without changing its character. Plus, we need all the room we have for exhibits and now we are adding a new one."

As Hannah arranged her research she heard a woman talking with the volunteer at the information desk. Looking up she recognized Abby Wiley, a young energetic red head.

Abby had a big smile for Hannah and Izzy.

"I am so glad to see you," said Hannah. "I thought you weren't going to start on this project until September since you are busy waitressing."

"That's true. But today is my day off. Izzy thought it would be a good idea to touch base with you early in the project. I can learn what you have discovered and start thinking about how to set up the display this fall."

Hannah explained she had clear evidence that two restaurants in town had been moved from the island as well as some houses near the harbor.

"I am finding that the best way to verify which buildings were moved is when the present owners have some kind of documentation. Brocton told me his shop and Lydia's were connected as one building, when they were on Billingsgate. They were moved together. He says he is searching his files for some old photos showing the building being floated."

There was general agreement that the project was off to a good start and Abby began to get excited about the possibility that Brocton had photos.

Izzy told them that the museum had photos. "I know we have photos and documentation in the museum archives. It will take some time going through things since we have a wealth of material here but much of it is not well organized."

The two women left the museum together. Across the street outside the Pirate's Pub Hannah spotted Armand who was leaning against his jeep talking and laughing with Svetlana, a young woman from Eastern Europe, who worked at the deli. His shirt was unbuttoned revealing a bronzed chest. His bleached blond hair was unruly as usual. It was all part of the package thought Hannah.

Svetlana greeted them, but Armand who was usually suave abruptly left without making any of his usual flirtatious remarks.

"That is unlike Armand," said Hannah. "He usually loves to strut in front of women."

"I am afraid it is because of me," said Abby. "Brocton is carrying my work in his gallery this summer and Armand is furious. He feels that his work is far superior and was insulted that his work would be in the same gallery with mine."

"I heard about that," said Hannah sympathetically. "Armand decided to rent space from Lola to show his art."

"Mr. DeCristo just invited me to see his paintings," said Svetlana obviously smitten.

Hannah laughed saying, "Svetlana, he wants all the nice looking young women to see his paintings."

Saying good-bye she headed for the library. "Perhaps I should have warned Svetlana about Armand," she thought guiltily. "If she goes to his house to see his paintings he definitely will make a pass at her." Then she dismissed this telling herself that Svetlana was a big girl and able to take care of herself.

At the library while walking through the book stacks making some selections, Hannah saw Troy Oliver sitting at a desk in a quiet corner typing furiously on his laptop. She did not disturb him but as she checked out her books she asked Cindy, one of the librarians, if he worked often at the library.

"I think he comes a few days a week," she answered. "There are a lot of writers in Oyster Town, especially in the summer, and many of them spend some time working on their books here."

"I know of at least two people who've done some writing here," Hannah said and mentioned a well-known British broadcaster who thanked the Oyster Town library in the forward of one of his books. "Also one of my neighbors who is a scientist mentioned the library in one of his recent books."

Chapter 9

"Hannah, are you ready? We have a two o'clock start," Martin called as he gathered sails, the dingy oars and other paraphernalia they needed for sailing.

Hannah appeared and asked what the predicted wind velocity was.

"Light winds which will make you happy. It should be a nice day to race. The winds are light but steady and it is sunny but not too warm."

They drove to the end of the street where they moored their sailboat, *Windswept*, in a small cove which was part of Bog Bay. Doc, who also raced in the weekly regatta, had already set sail from Lieutenant Island and they could see his boat in the distance.

"Doc is already in Billingsgate Bay," Martin mused. "Maybe we should have gotten off earlier. With today's tide we could have gotten out of Bog Bay and Grampus Creek by noon."

It was indeed a beautiful day to sail and Hannah thought that for once she might be relaxed during the races. She found that things happened so quickly while racing that much of what she and Martin did was based on instinct. Martin often said that he was happy she crewed for him since they anticipated each others actions and the movement of the boat.

"This is a surprise," said Hannah as they approached the start. "The committee boat has already set up the course. They are actually early for a change."

Martin was practicing various maneuvers and

sizing up the competition. The usual group was assembled: Doc in *Patients* with Ben, Sue and Lou, two sisters whom the others had nicknamed The Nuns, in their boat *Gumdrop*, Gerard with his cousin in *Racer* and Ted and his son in *Salty*. Two other boats also joined the regatta.

Gerard came alongside *Windswept* and hollered, "Do you know anything about the new competition?"

Martin answered in the negative and added, "They look like pretty good sailors. This will add to the excitement."

Martin maneuvered his boat close to the committee boat to learn the course layout for the first race. Hannah laughed. "Look at the committee boat. The kids resurrected the little cannon this year."

Sure enough on the bow of the boat the teenagers had placed a small cannon.

Shortly afterwards they heard a boom. Martin immediately looked at his watch. The boom from the cannon meant the first race would start in three minutes.

"We should use a flag to announce the course but then this isn't Newport," said Martin.

"No, but we do have a canon," replied Hannah.

Warnings were given at two minutes then one minute. The seven boats were jockeying for position at the start.

"A good start on a starboard tact is crucial in any race," said Martin. "But it is especially important in ours since our course is so short."

Martin hovered close to the starting line being careful not to cross it too soon. He did this by letting his sails luff. With 10 seconds to the start he ordered Hannah to pull in the jib sail and he pulled in the main sail. They crossed the starting line just as the cannon boomed out the start of the race.

The course was a triangle and Hannah and Martin led all the way. As they crossed the finish line to yet another cannon boom Hannah said, "That is the way I like to race. Ahead the whole time with no challenges."

Three more races followed. One of the newcomers won the second race, and Martin cursed as he finished fifth. The third was a close race with The Nuns edging out Martin for first. The last ended in a fiasco. Four boats were contending for first place as they approached the finish line – *Racer*, *Patients*, *Windswept, and Salty*.

"Gerard's tack has him heading for the committee boat. It won't take him across the finish line," Martin said to Hannah. "He will have to jibe. That will put him out of contention. I think Ted may be in the best position to win. He will make it across the finish line just in front of the committee boat."

Martin finished speaking when the teenagers on the committee boat started to scream. Gerard had attempted to cross the line in front of the boat but instead crashed into it and his stern swung around and hit Ted's boat. No one was hurt but there were scrapes and gouges in all three boats.

Patients crossed as the winner but angry words were exchanged and protests were filed. The teenagers were visibly upset so Ben took control. He gestured for everyone to stop arguing and called out that they should meet at the yacht club in two hours.

Two hours later they all gathered on the deck of the club where Gerard looked chagrined and offered to buy everyone a drink and to pay for any repairs.

"I am happy to see that Gerard accepts full responsibility for the collision," said Ben. "There is no way he can escape this time."

In the past the racers found that Gerard violated rules but then found, or as Hannah said 'made up' a rule to exonerate himself.

Ted had calmed down and told Gerard that the collision was a good excuse for him to do some work on his boat. "It has needed it for some time so this is a good reason to finally get it done. But I imagine the yacht club will want you to pay for repairs to the committee boat."

"And an apology and a gift for the kids would be a nice gesture," Ben added. "They were a bit shaken up."

"Gerard doesn't apologize easily." The group turned to see Maddie walking up the steps to the deck." She cackled and added, "It isn't in his nature."

Gerard gave her a wary look. "What are you doing here?' he asked abruptly.

"Same thing as you," she replied holding up a glass of wine.

"Don't be so nervous, Gerard. I won't tell your secrets." Maddie teased.

"You're crazy," Gerard muttered.

"Ah!" Maddie whispered to Hannah. "Lots of big egos. These are all part of Oyster Town's secrets. Everyone has secrets and I know most of them. Billingsgate buildings, art work, gallery owners, writers, big egos."

Hannah asked her to explain but Maddie gave a laugh, shook her head and said, "Come see me. Make it worth my while and I'll tell you some secrets."

Chapter 10

Early Sunday morning Hannah and Martin finished a quick breakfast and gathered their gear for clamming. On Wednesdays and Sundays during the summer, people who had non-commercial shellfish licenses could collect oysters and dig for clams during low tide in the area near the marina jetty. Martin put their clamming rakes and buckets in the Volvo while Hannah pinned her license onto a baseball cap. Martin also put on a carpenters apron in which he kept some old screwdrivers.

"Everyone has his own quirks when clamming and oystering," said Martin. "I like to use this apron because if I find some legal size oysters my screwdriver will come in handy to scrape off the attached spat."

By law any oysters one collected had to be three inches long to be legal and all spat removed. Spat were tiny oysters and spat attached to a variety of things – rocks, docks, and other oysters. It was not easy to remove them and though others had their methods Martin found a screwdriver most effective.

It was eight o'clock, an hour before low tide and already there were several cars in the large parking lot. As usual the Brewsters headed to a section about 400 feet from the jetty. Martin waded into deeper water while Hannah was uncertain about what she would do. She was unsure of her clamming techniques.

Martin reminded her again. "Rake over an area. If you feel some resistance and a smooth scraping sound it is probably a clam. Go under it and pull up."

"That's easy for you to say," she answered glumly. Then she brightened up. "Actually I am hoping that the new rake you bought me for my birthday will help." Hannah's new rake had smaller tongs and was much lighter.

"If you hit a particularly rich area call me," she said as Martin headed into deeper water.

More and more people arrived but everyone knew the etiquette of clamming was to stay out of someone else's space. Hannah had raked a wide area without any luck. She could see Martin steadily collecting clams so she decided to move to a new area. After a few minutes she began to get lucky. She felt the resistance, the smooth shape and within a half hour had collected nearly half a bucket of clams.

By that time Martin had gotten his quota for the week, a full bucket.

"I think we have enough clams," he said showing her his basket and looking at hers. She agreed but stopped here and there to rake for a few more clams.

As she followed Martin out of the water a shellfish warden approached them on his moped especially designed to drive over sand. He asked for their names and license numbers.

Recognizing the names he asked if they were Jeff's parents. "Jeff frequently stops by the office to see if there is anything he can write about for *The Chronicle*. I also go to hear him when he plays at the Sand Bar."

The warden looked into their buckets to see that the clams were legal size and noted the amount they had gathered. "You have your limit for the week Mr. Brewster," he said. "But Mrs. Brewster you can get another half basket on Wednesday."

Hannah smiled at him and said sweetly, "All I wanted was half a bucket." As they walked to the car she muttered to Martin, "He didn't have to rub it in that I only had half my quota."

"Come on Hannah," said Martin. "He didn't mean it that way. Look around there are lots of people who don't have a full bucket and don't want one."

"Really," she said. "You never leave unless you have a full bucket. It is like a badge of honour for you to walk across the beach to the parking lot holding up a full bucket, swaggering with pride. Then you come home and I've got all these clams to deal with!"

"Hannah, that's not fair. You know I help out. I wash all the clams and steam the large ones."

"True, but I make the baked stuffed quahogs and clam chowder and…."

Martin interrupted her by pointing across the bay. In the distance they could see a group of people gathered on the flats.

"That area is not opened to seasonal shellfishing," said Martin. "And there are too many people to be working on a commercial grant."

As a matter of fact," added Hannah, "that is close to where Ben has his grant."

Then from a distance they heard the wail of sirens and saw the red and blue lights of a police car.

"Something is going on over there," Martin said. "I wonder if someone got hurt working on his grant."

"Or had a heart attack," mused Hannah.

When they arrived home Jeff's dilapidated truck was in the driveway and they found him in Martin's office with his ear to the phone, typing furiously. Having Jeff sometimes work from their home meant they learned about news before it went to print.

"A body was found on the flats, on Ben's grant in Bog Bay," he told them cupping the phone. "I'm talking with Santos who is briefing me."

Anxious to know the details but realizing they had to wait until Jeff was finished they decided to deal with the clams they had harvested. Martin separated them according to size. Some were littlenecks which they would eat raw with spicy cocktail sauce. Others were cherrystones which they would cook with garlic, parsley and olive oil and add to pasta, shells and all. Finally there were the quahogs which Martin started to steam on the burner of their grill. These Hannah would grind and use for baked stuffed quahogs made with chopped onion, peppers, spicy Portuguese linguica, and bread crumbs. She would also freeze some to use later in clam chowder.

As they worked they checked to see if Jeff was finished and ready to give them more details. Just as Hannah felt she had no patience left there was a knock on their sliding glass door and as it slid open Ben appeared. He looked a bit shaken. Martin offered him a beer and the three of them went to the deck where from a distance they could see Ben's grant. Now there were only a few people on the grant and all were dressed in black. Hannah assumed they must be police officers.

Ben took a sip of his beer and told the Brewsters what had happened.

"This morning I was helping Charley on his grant. I could spare the time because I had hired my nephew, Joe, to work with me this summer. I saw Joe pull up and park his truck just off the beach and walk to my grant. A few minutes later I glanced over and he was acting strangely, as if he was sick. It took me a few minutes to walk from Charley's grant to mine and when I got there he was sitting with his cell phone in his hand but too sick to use it."

"Poor kid," said Martin. "I imagine he found the body."

"Yes. I assumed that you would know there was a body since Jeff works for the paper. That is partly why I stopped by. I had to talk to someone but didn't want to be the one to spread the news. That can wait until the police and press are ready to make the announcement."

The Brewsters made sympathetic sounds and Ben continued.

"I walked over to what looked like a pile of rags lying on one corner of the grant. The cloth was caught on some of the shellfish paraphernalia."

"At first I thought it was just a clump of clothing but a closer look revealed a body. Poor Joe. The body wasn't a pretty sight. It must have been in the water a few hours and the crabs had already gotten to the eyes and soft skin of the nose, lips and ears."

Hannah felt a little sick herself but asked if he knew who it was.

"From the clothes and what was left of the face I think it was Mad Maddie," he replied.

"Oh no!" breathed Hannah.

At that moment Jeff rushed out of the office. "Yes. It was Maddie," he confirmed. "I am off to the police station. I will see if Miyu can come to dinner here tonight. Maybe she'll be able to give us more information."

"Let's have a variety of clams casino, baked stuffed quahogs and a salad for dinner," said Hannah. "We can do the clams casino on the grill so it will be informal. Do you mind going to the bistro and picking up a baguette and to the deli for some olives and cheese?" she asked Martin.

"A few minutes later Martin manoeuvred the MG into a parking space behind town hall and walked to the deli. Just outside he saw a local shellfisherman deep in conversation with Moses Paine, one of the town's selectmen. They nodded to Martin as he joined them.

"Come on, you can tell me. Did Maddie commit suicide? Was it a boating accident?" the man pressed the selectman.

"Honestly, I don't know anything yet. The body has just left for the morgue and an autopsy. All this is in the hands of the police. It could be a few days before we know anything."

At the lumberyard where Martin had an errand to run he heard two builders discussing the news in the parking lot.

"Remember the murder last summer," said Smithies, a well known developer.

"Yeah that shocked the town," the other man replied putting out a cigarette. "Poor Petey, but I guess he deserved it."

"Well maybe we have another murder on our hands," said Smithies lowering his voice so Martin had a hard time hearing without moving closer. "Maddie went around town talking about secrets and knowing all of them. Everyone heard her. Well, maybe someone wanted to silence her."

That evening Miyu arrived at the Brewsters in a pair of tan shorts and pale yellow blouse. Her long black hair fell down her shoulders and back. Slim and only 5 feet tall she did not look at all like a police officer, let alone a police chief. Her wan smile made her look even younger. "We certainly aren't celebrating anything," she said softly, "but I brought champagne anyway."

Jeff arrived at that moment. He went to shower. Martin opened the champagne and Hannah and Miyu started chopping garlic, red peppers, shallots and pancetta for the clams casino.

"The whole town is talking about Maddie's death," announced Jeff as he dried his hair.

"I know," replied his father. "When I was in town it was the topic of every conversation I heard or overheard. Smithies thought it might be murder."

They all looked at Miyu to see if she would reveal anything about Maddie's death.

"Well," urged Jeff. "Are you going to tell us what the police have learned?" he asked putting his arm around her.

She laughed and looked as if she was starting to relax. "The truth is we are not sure what was the cause of death. I did ask Doc to look at the body even though this is a bit irregular. I wanted a doctor to look at the body before it was taken away. She could have been walking or wading, tripped and hit her head. She could have fallen out of her boat and hit her head. We are looking for an abandoned boat along the beaches."

"Someone mentioned suicide," said Martin.

"We haven't ruled that out," said Miyu. "Honestly we won't know until there is an autopsy."

"Remember Lt. Connolly from the state police?" she asked.

"I sure do," said Jeff. "He is the good looking dude who last summer was very interested in getting to know you better."

"Yes," she looked up at him slyly. "He is very handsome but we never got the chance to know each other very well. Maybe this summer?" she teased Jeff. "Lt Connolly is arriving late tonight and technically he will be in charge of this case if there is any foul play."

"We worked with him last year. Invite him to Jeff's for breakfast," encouraged Hannah. "We'll bring fruit, coffee, croissants, and bagels. It will be our way of welcoming him back."

"Our way of staying on his good side, you mean," laughed Martin.

Chapter 11

The sound of the phone ringing awoke Hannah and Martin early the next day. It was a business call for Martin. Hannah busied herself organizing the coffee and fruit for breakfast at Jeff's. When she finished Martin was still on the phone so she watered her vegetable and flower gardens. Things were coming along nicely.

When Hannah returned to the house Martin was still busy on the phone. She tiptoed into his office and handed him a note saying she was going to town to buy croissants and bagels and that she would meet him at Jeff's. He nodded and gave her a wave.

At the last minute she decided to pack her bathing suit. It was a warm morning and a swim in the pond at Jeff's would feel good.

She was one of the first customers at the bistro where she spoke with the young French baker trying out the French she had acquired a few years ago while living in France. She then went on to buy bagels at the deli. A few minutes later she was driving down the dirt road behind Bayberry Inn to Jeff's house. Jeff's truck was in the drive. He was nowhere to be seen and she decided he was still asleep. Hannah quietly organized things for breakfast, put on her bathing suit, and dove into the cool, clear water of the pond. Martin arrived a half hour later just as she was finishing her swim and Jeff was exiting the outdoor shower.

"Hi!" she called out to them. "Everything is set for breakfast. I've just got to change and dry my hair."

They were sitting on Jeff's deck drinking coffee when Miyu arrived with Lt. Connolly in a state police vehicle. Lt. Connolly was the archetype state policeman. He was tall, dark, muscular but trim, wearing aviator type sunglasses. He was also very good looking.

Over breakfast Lt. Connolly said that he would hold a press conference on Maddie's death that morning but there was little new information to announce.

"It is really quite frustrating," he said. "There is a fairly new, very adequate medical examiner's facility in Falmouth but because of budget cuts at the state level it is hardly used. I was there two weeks ago out of curiosity and found boxes of medical equipment unopened."

"What that means," interjected Miyu, "is medical examiners have to travel from Boston to Cape Cod to examine bodies and then bring them to the facilities in Boston for an internal or external autopsy. If the facility in Falmouth were available it would save travel time."

"How long does it take to arrange an autopsy?" asked Hannah.

"It could be a few weeks," Connolly answered. "When there is a death from natural or unnatural causes that call for further investigation a medical examiner, who is specially trained in these things, is assigned to look into the death. Sometimes only an external examination is enough to determine the cause of death but other times an internal autopsy is needed."

"Do you think there will be an internal autopsy on Maddie?" Jeff asked, now taking notes.

"Probably," Lt. Connolly answered cautiously. "One thing though. Valuable time is being lost. A medical examiner can tell us lots of things about a body at the early stages of an investigation. The longer we have to wait before a medical examiner looks at the body the more our investigation slows down and perhaps evidence gets lost."

Miyu and the state policeman rose thanking them for breakfast, saying they needed to get to the press conference. Jeff, too, started to head toward his beat-up truck.

"One thing I must say," said Lt. Connolly smiling at Miyu. "Chief Lee did a smart thing asking your friend, Doc, to look at the body before it was shipped to Boston. He is not a medical examiner but he is a doctor and his examination may give us some ideas on how to proceed in this case. Otherwise, all we can do is ask people about seeing or hearing anything suspicious on the water last night or early this the morning and look for an abandoned boat."

He beamed at the young police chief and added, "Now if I can convince her to join the state police and come to Boston."

If Jeff heard this remark he showed no reaction.

The afternoon found Hannah and Martin in *Windswept* sailing over what at low tide would be the remains of Billingsgate Island. "We were supposed to sail out here today to visit the island at low tide. Maddie's death changed those plans," she mused. Then she continued, "My project for the Captain Kendrick House Museum is coming along nicely. When the tides are right again we need to come here at low tide so you can take photos. All I need is a little bit more research and those photos."

"That's good news," said Martin, "because I was going to ask you if you wanted to go back to London with me for a few days."

Hannah who was sitting on the gunwales since the boat was heeling, nearly fell into the water. "What do you mean?"

"The phone call I got this morning was from Giles Cuthbright. I worked with him on a project a few years ago. He called to ask me if I was available to work on something that has just come up."

"And you said yes without consulting me?"

"Hannah," he replied calmly. "I am a working man. Since you retired I am the breadwinner."

Hannah knew he was teasing her but it also irked her. "You are not a full time working man. You are supposed to be cutting back, retiring as a matter of fact. And I do earn some money from time to time as a consultant."

She paused then said, "Well, tell me about it."

"Giles called and told me that his organization received a grant to make records from private Victorian cemeteries in London better organized, more accessible. He asked if I would be interested in creating an electronic data base for them. I only need to be in London for a few days to discuss the project. After that I can do most of the work from the Cape."

"I guess it sounds interesting," said Hannah. "At least it is something I understand, unlike corporate data bases."

"Actually you might be able to make some suggestions to make the data base user friendly. Giles hopes I can make it easier for people to do research on their families or just do research in general and that is right up your alley."

"Speaking of research," Hannah said coyly. "I, too, was contacted about a consultancy job. Just before we left London, Gemma and Trudy asked me to help them revise the research and writing package we created for students a few years ago. Apparently a publishing company is interested in buying it, but it needs updating."

"Do you want to do it?" Martin asked.

"When they approached me, I was disappointed that the timing was wrong for me. This is a project that I feel keenly about and I have been thinking about possible changes and improvements over the last few weeks," Hannah replied. "Yes, I would like to work on this and like you I probably need only a day or two to do my part."

"Plus you have enjoyed working with Gemma and Trudy in the past," Martin added.

She warmed to the idea. "They are both excellent teachers, and we drew on our teaching experience when we created the writing package. It would be fun and interesting."

"Okay, then we should head home so I can look into flights," said Martin as he changed tack and headed toward Bog Bay and their mooring.

Chapter 12

It was just after dawn when Hannah and Martin finished a quick breakfast and prepared themselves for a bike ride.

"Where do you want to go?" Martin asked Hannah.

"Let's see," she considered some of their options. "We could do Marconi Beach and Marconi Site or the Ocean View Drive loop. If we do that we could stop to swim at the pond. Or we could do some of the fire roads in the National Park."

"You know we haven't done the ride to Nauset Lighthouse this summer. We are off early so it might be a good choice," Martin suggested.

This ride went along the bike path of the Cape Cod Rail Trail until Nauset Road and then Cable Road leading to Nauset Light Beach. From there it continued to Coast Guard Beach and then on the National Seashore bike path to Salt Pond Visitors Center and back to the rail trail.

"Okay let's do that loop. It is about fifteen miles so without too many stops we should be done before it gets warm," Hannah said. She then added, "But we will have to stop to look at the ocean at Nauset Light Beach and the marsh at Coast Guard Beach."

About two hours later they re-crossed Route 6, rode down Bog Bay Road and turned into their dirt driveway.

"I think I am going to either take a nap this afternoon or go sit on the beach with a book," Hannah said removing her bike helmet and wiping the sweat from her forehead. "But first I am going to shower then organize myself for London. What time is our flight tomorrow?"

"We are taking a British Air day flight which leaves Logan at 8:50 am and arrives at Heathrow at 8:40 pm," was his reply.

"That makes an early morning start tomorrow," she groaned. "We will have to leave here at 4:30 in the morning to get to the airport by 6:30."

Martin laughed at her pained look. "We can leave at 4:30 or we can leave tonight and stay near the airport. A number of hotels allow you to leave your car in their lot for free for up to a week. And they have shuttles that take you to the airport. So if we stay overnight we will save money on parking. And actually all this would be on my expense account anyway. So do you want to leave tonight?"

It was agreed that they would leave by five that evening. "I'd better get going," said Hannah. "I have to pack and arrange for someone to water the garden at least once."

Hannah was busy packing a small suitcase when Martin came into the bedroom. "Troy Oliver just phoned. He is having problems with his computer. He thinks he has lost some files and asked if I could help him recover them."

"Can you help?" Hannah asked.

"I am pretty certain that I can. Usually these things are pretty straightforward. But do you mind packing for me in case it takes more time than I think it will? I will need a suit and at least two shirts. Otherwise just casual things."

Hannah grinned at him. "You know I don't mind packing for you. It means I have control over what you take. None of your old slouchy pants and t-shirts!"

A few minutes later Martin parked his car in front of a three-quarter Cape house just above Commercial Street. "How do you like living here in the center of town?" Martin asked as Troy opened the front door. "Hannah and I often think it would be nice being in town. We feel we might take advantage of activities if we were closer. Like going to gallery openings more often."

Troy answered that being on his own he preferred being closer to town. "I spend a lot of time writing at the library and that is only a few minutes away. But I wasn't able to get a mooring let alone a slip at the harbour for my new boat. There is quite a long waiting list. So I have to drive to get to my boat. I am keeping it at the landing just south of the Yacht Club."

Troy ushered Martin into a small room at the back where he had created a study. "My publishing company asked me to write a few reviews for them. I don't know where I get the time since I am so busy writing my own mysteries but the money is good. Anyway I seem to have deleted one of the files accidentally. Can you help me get it back? Some of the stuff needed major revision but there were some files that I was ready to send to my publisher."

"You're lucky. If this happened tomorrow I wouldn't be here. Hannah and I are going to London on business for a few days," Martin told the writer.

Troy enthused about London, telling Martin that the main setting for his newest book was London.

Martin sat down at the desk and began to work on the computer. "If I search through the hard drive I think I can recover your file once you give me the name. It will probably take an hour or so."

While Martin was busy with Troy Oliver, Hannah brought perishables from her fridge to Jeff's. As she turned the corner to drive to his house, she saw him standing with Lola in her small backyard surrounded by furniture, old tools, old toys – a general mess. She drove to his house, put the food she had brought into his fridge and walked back to Lola's

"What is going on here?" she asked incredulously, looking at the piles that covered the entire area.

Lola was so angry she could hardly speak. She had her hands on the hips of her short shorts and her ample chest was heaving under her tight blouse. "That Brocton," she spit out his name. "He told me he would help me clean out the basement and look! This is what he left me with." Her eyes were like daggers.

Jeff interrupted knowing his explanation would be clearer and shorter. He explained that Brocton worked on the basement for only a few hours.

"If even that," Lola interjected.

Jeff tried to calm her down and then continued talking to his mother.

"Brocton seemed eager to help Lola clear out the basement. Lydia used to store lots of pieces for her antique shop there and it really got packed. He said he thought he might want to buy a few items and had some friends who might also be interested in buying things. He also was going to arrange for a friend to take things on consignment. Basically he was going to help Lola get rid of the stuff so Armand could use it as a storage space."

"Yes, I know all about this," his mother replied, and though she didn't say it, she thought Lola was naïve if she believed Brocton. Why would he want to make things easy for Armand when the two men were feuding?

"Oh Jeff!" Lola moaned, looking forlorn. "What if it rains? Things will get ruined. You have to help me."

Jeff sighed, "Okay, Lola. Here's the deal. You go get some beer and pizzas. I'll call some of my friends and we will get going on this."

Lola hugged him giving him an extra tight squeeze. She then turned to Hannah and pointed to an oak end table. "Armand said he wanted to buy this. It will fit in the Volvo. Will you take it to his house? You can leave it on his porch if he isn't at home." Before Hannah could answer she was off.

"I don't know how she does it," Hannah said to Jeff. "Somehow, somebody bails her out of her predicaments."

When Hannah left with the piece of furniture in her car, Jeff was trying to organize the chaos. Some he would donate; some bring to the dump; most would go back in the cellar.

"Lola can tell Armand he can live without storage space," he muttered as he carried an antique Windsor chair back to the basement."

Hannah felt a little uneasy as she drove down the sand path leading to the bay beach and Armand's low slung cottage. She didn't trust him but said to herself, "He probably won't be at home, and I can just drop the table off and leave."

Hannah parked at what was the back of the house since the front was literally on the beach with the front porch and door facing the water. It was a beautiful spot.

"No one would ever be allowed to build here today. Too close to the water," she thought to herself. She knew that when Armand bought the house he had to follow all kinds of regulations about renovating the building and had to install a special septic system.

The table was solid oak so a bit heavy and she struggled in the soft sand. As she approached the porch a young, very pretty woman in a strapless sundress descended the steps and started down the beach. Hannah did not know her and was about to say something as a greeting when Armand called to her from the house.

"Hannah, put down that table. I'll carry it. Come sit on the porch."

Hannah sat on the steps while Armand collected his furniture. Then he dropped to her side. "This is a pleasant surprise," he purred. "You know I always welcome your company."

Hannah mumbled something about having to leave but he put his hand on her shoulder and laughed, "You can spare a few minutes, I know you can." He shifted and Hannah felt he was invading her space. "I am still searching for the perfect model for my abstract nudes. Mona is quite good," he said looking at the receding back of the woman who had just left. "But I think I want someone with a little more maturity. Someone who may be smouldering inside. That is what I want to capture." He then cupped the nape of her neck and added "And I want a brunette, just your hair shade."

"Stop it Armand!" Hannah said a little breathless. "You are teasing me and I don't like it." She got up and started to walk to her car.

"I am not teasing you," he called after her. "I mean it. You may be my ideal model."

Hannah quickened her pace and was sure Armand was laughing at her graceless departure. Back in the car she cursed herself for being foolish enough to go to Armand's alone. An almost identical exchange had happened last summer when she was alone with him. "I should know better and Martin would be furious," she scolded herself vowing not to tell her husband about the encounter.

Upon returning home Hannah packed a small lunch and drove to the ocean beach where she relaxed and read. She put down her book since it didn't hold her interest and thought about Maddie. Hannah had some reservations about leaving at the start of the investigation into her death, but she told herself it may be a week before the medical examiner releases any information and they were only going to London for a few days. She also thought about Armand and how forward he could be.

"I don't know if he is kidding or seeing how far he can get," she said to herself, "but in any case I should not go to his house alone."

It was a perfect beach day and Hannah had to force herself to leave. When she climbed the path to the parking lot she was surprised to see Doc. "Isn't it unusual for you to be on the Cape during the week? I thought you were here only on the weekends."

"This summer I decided to spend more time in Oyster Town. I am taking three and sometimes four day weekends. I must say I am enjoying it."

Hannah wasn't certain she should broach the topic of Maddie but curiosity got the best of her. "Miyu told us that you examined Maddie's body." Then quickly added that Lt. Connolly praised her for doing so because it meant someone with medical knowledge saw the body soon after death.

"Apparently, a medical examiner may not get to the body for a week or so and the police feel that affects an investigation."

Doc agreed with her and added, "I don't mind telling you what I found since I know you often get inside information on police cases through Jeff and keep it confidential. There was some bruising along the carotid artery."

"You mean Maddie may have been choked," said Hannah aghast.

"All I am saying is that it looked suspicious to me. I am not sure how Chief Lee and Lt Connolly will proceed on what I told them. They probably will want corroboration from the medical examiner before announcing anything."

A few hours later she and Martin were crossing the Sagamore Bridge leaving the Cape and heading toward Boston. Hannah told Martin about Doc's news but kept her visit to Armand to herself. They drove in silence, each contemplated the possibility that Maddie had been murdered.

They checked into the hotel and were joined for dinner by Jeff who was going to Boston for an evening awards ceremony. He had won first place for a human interest story he had written for *The Cape Chronicle*.

"I was surprised when I won since I didn't think it was the best thing I'd ever written," he said. Then added, "I am in the small, community newspaper category so maybe there weren't too many selections to choose from."

"It doesn't matter," said his mother. "The critics who selected you liked it. Dad and I are proud of you."

Martin agreed then said, "Speaking of critics, this morning when I was restoring a file Troy Oliver had inadvertently deleted, I saw some of the reviews he told me he was writing. From what I saw they were negative and sarcastic."

"How does this guy find the time to write so many mysteries, plus do critiques? I have trouble doing a few articles a week for *The Chronicle*."

Martin and Hannah exchanged glances. "You know, Jeff," said his father, "some people work a full week. They don't organize their lives around surfing conditions."

Jeff had heard this before and answered in his usual manner. "A reporter needs to be out and about to pick up stories. They don't come by sitting at home in front of a computer. Besides the story that won the award is a surfing story about a family where four generations surf together."

Martin and Hannah couldn't disagree with that.

Hannah returned to the topic of Troy Oliver. "He does seem like a prolific writer," she said. "Writing must come very easily to him."

"Actually, I thought the reviews were rather poorly written, a bit sloppy. From what I could see he used a pseudonym for some," Martin said. Then a few minutes later remarked, "I have an idea that I am going to check when we get back to our room."

Jeff said his goodbyes, "Thanks for the dinner and have a good trip."

"He managed another free meal on his parents," Martin said shaking his head.

Just before Jeff left the room he turned back and called to his mother, "How did it go at Armand's this afternoon? Did he behave like a gentleman?"

Hannah gave him an exasperated look and when Martin began to ask, she said with her teeth gritted, "Don't ask. I don't want to talk about it."

When they returned to their room Martin spent some time on the computer. Finally he called to Hannah. "Come see this. It is very interesting."

What Martin found were severa caustic reviews of books on the Amazon.com website.

"I checked under the pseudonym he used. He has written lots and lots of reviews. They are long and he seems to target new writers. He certainly is blunt and critical. This looks a lot like the stuff I found in his files."

"So he isn't writing official reviews for his publishing company," said Hannah surprised. "Why would he want to spend his time writing these?" Looking from the reviews to her husband she said, "You would think he was busy enough churning out his books."

"I don't know," responded Martin. "Maybe it's an ego trip."

Chapter 13

The flight to London was uneventful and soon they were on the Paddington Express for the 15 minute train journey into London. Hannah observed the other passengers who like herself were weary from travelling. One young woman especially caught her interest. She was struggling with a very large suitcase and an almost equally large backpack and was relieved when she finally hauled everything onto the train and fell into a seat. Arriving at Paddington Station, Hannah found herself walking next to the burdened young woman who turned to her and asked directions to the tube station.

"Where are you going?" Hannah asked, concerned about how the woman was going to get all of her luggage onto the tube.

"I am going to the Bloomsbury area, near the British Museum. I just arrived and I am going to be a student at Birkbeck College. I have student housing in that area," was her reply.

Martin then joined the conversation and said that most of the tube stations had some stairs she would have to climb and that it might be better to take a taxi. The woman seemed a bit concerned and Martin added, "The fare should be about £10 to £12 and will get you exactly where you want to go. You don't want to be wandering around looking for addresses at this hour."

"That doesn't sound too expensive," the young woman replied. "Everyone back home warned me that taxis in London were very expensive."

"They aren't cheap," was Martin's answer, "but sometimes the expense is worth it."

The woman walked with them to the taxi rank outside the station. There was a long queue but it moved quickly as taxis descended on the station. Most were the familiar black color but some were in the newer shades of blue, white, and yellow.

"Oh dear!" the woman moaned as she calculated that the taxi meant for her was a yellow one. "I was told only to take black ones."

Hannah was about to get into their taxi when she quickly explained that the warning was about taking private, unlicensed taxis. "You will soon learn the distinctive shape of the licensed ones. They all used to be black but now come in various colors. Good luck with your studies."

Hannah sat back and turned to Martin. "In a few weeks she will be getting around like a Londoner. It is the first few days that are difficult."

The next morning since there was no food in the flat Hannah went in search of coffee, fruit, and bread for breakfast. When she returned she found Martin on the computer.

"We got an email from Jeff telling us what the police found in Maddie's cottage. Come take a look."

The email contained an attachment with photos of the items which included news clippings on Gerard Marceau and Brocton Phillips, photos of paintings, Troy Oliver's books, several decks of Tarot cards, a wedding band, and a spiral notebook with poems and snatches of poetry, probably written by Maddie.

In the email Jeff explained that Miyu was trying to make sense of the objects and that she was also questioning people who might have heard sounds from the bay on the night Maddie died.

"Lt. Connolly is back in Boston pending the autopsy report so she is able to conduct the investigation on her own with her own officers," Jeff wrote. "Gotta sign off. I am giving Lola some surfing lessons in the afternoon. Miyu is coming over after work for a swim and dinner. It has gotten very hot here – in the high 80s."

"I don't know what puzzles me more, Jeff's relationship with Lola and Miya or the objects found at Maddie's." Hannah sighed as Martin shut down the computer.

It was a nice morning and they were both early for their appointments. They walked to South End Green where Martin continued on to the tube. Hannah took the C-11 bus to Swiss Cottage where she had a number of bus options going toward Baker Street. Instead of meeting at the international school where she had worked for a number of years with Gemma and Trudy, they were meeting in a Nash terrace house on the edge of Regent's Park. It was a new purchase by the school, and was a venue for a variety of events including receptions, small concerts, student art shows, and a place for off-campus meetings.

From the bus Hannah admired the white stucco terraces that fringed the park. They were built in the early 19th century when George IV was Prince Regent. He acted in this capacity when his father, George III suffered from mental illness.

She got off at the Alpha Close stop and walked north. Gemma and Trudy were waiting for her at the entrance to an elegant Regency building and after signing in with the security guard and taking a brief tour of the building, they settled into a large handsome room equipped with all the technology of a modern conference room. They spent the first half hour catching up on personal things before tackling the task at hand.

"We are still waiting for a decision from the school as to whether this writing package is our intellectual property or the property of the school since it was written while we were on sabbatical," said Gemma as she connected her laptop to the LCD projector so they could see the files on the large screen.

"It really doesn't matter at the moment who owns this package," added Trudy. "What we want to do is review and revise it so that it is acceptable to the textbook company that is interested in purchasing it. They are paying us to do the work over the next few days."

They enjoyed working together and by late afternoon decided they had accomplished enough for the day.

"I think we should be able to finish up by noon tomorrow and then Trudy and I will take the package to school where we will go over parts of it with some students. They are taking a writing course as part of summer school," Gemma said.

"We have chosen students who learned research and writing techniques through this program, and we will see what they think of the main changes we have made," Trudy explained. "Then we can spend Saturday morning making any alterations and doing the final polishing."

"So shall we go to the pub and celebrate our good work?" Hannah asked.

It was warm and sunny and they were lucky to find an outside table sheltered by a large umbrella. Hannah started to tell them about Maddie's death. When she got to the part about what was found in her cottage Gemma said, "Do you have the photos of the paintings in your email?"

"Yes," she replied. "Jeff sent the email and attachments to both Martin and myself. Why?"

"I am curious to see if Trudy knows the paintings," was her reply.

"It is too bad I didn't mention this when we were working. We could have had the paintings projected on the large screen. It would have been easier to see them," said Hannah as she turned her laptop to Trudy.

Gemma and Hannah sipped their wine and chatted while Trudy studied the paintings. After several minutes she said, "Hannah, these are really interesting. All of these paintings are stolen art works."

"What!" Hannah said puzzled and surprised. "What do you mean?"

"All of these paintings were part of the art work looted by the Nazis during World War II and never recovered," Trudy answered and continued. "After the war the allies found most of the looted art. It had been stashed in places like salt mines, tunnels, and secluded castles. Even in places like the Jeu de Paume in Paris and Nazi headquarters in Munich. A lot of it, though, was never found. About 20% of the art stolen - over 100,000 pieces - was never returned to the rightful owners."

Gemma interrupted, "Trudy learned about this subject a few years ago when she took a course on stolen art at the Courtauld Institute."

"The hot topic at the time was whether museums had the moral responsibility to check their collections for looted art and return any pieces that had been stolen. I learned a lot about what was plundered, the work done to recover missing pieces, and the controversies surrounding the whole topic. There are publications which keep a register of stolen art items and some museums put their collection on websites especially to check if any pieces could have been Nazi loot. Today many dealers and galleries are more careful when they buy art."

"But," Gemma interjected, "other museums feel there should be a statute of limitations and if the original owner is now dead the item should remain with the museum. This is a topic that is as old as art itself. Who rightfully owns certain works of art? It always causes debate in my Western Civilization classes when we discuss the Elgin Marbles. Should they be returned to Greece or do they rightfully belong to the British Museum?"

"Yes, the students become quite animated on the subject giving strong arguments on both sides," Trudy said. "But to get back to your photos, all are documented as having disappeared during the war. With a little research I could tell you who the original owners were."

"I don't think I need that information, not now at least. But I will tell Chief Lee what you've told me," was Hannah's response.

"She probably knows the history of these paintings by now. It is easy to get this information on the internet," Trudy said as she finished her wine and prepared to leave.

The three women said their goodbyes, agreeing to meet early the next morning.

Before going home, Hannah decided to take the bus to Waterstones Bookstore on Hampstead High Street. As she walked to the large store, she recalled that the community had been very upset when this chain opened in this location, putting a popular and long standing independent store out of business.

"That was years ago," she thought to herself. "I wonder who remembers or cares today."

Then she looked up and down the street and realized that it was becoming a mini Oxford Street. More and more-high end chain stores were moving in as rents went up and independent stores could not afford to stay.

"Is this progress?" she thought.

Troy Oliver's book had a fairly prominent place in the window of the shop and at the counter. Troy had told her that the reviews from the British press were glowing and she wanted to read some. Hannah asked the cashier if he had any reviews of the book.

He handed her some photocopied papers. "They are very good. The critics applaud the book."

Hannah read through some and turned to the cashier. "Can I have these or at least borrow them for a day. I will return them sometime tomorrow."

The cashier shrugged his shoulders and said he didn't see why not. "You can have them. We have extra copies."

As she had hoped, Martin was at the flat when she returned. She told him what Trudy had said about the stolen art. "I will email Miyu," said Martin, "but I agree that she probably already has this information."

Hannah then showed him the reviews and said, "They praise the book." She read to him, "Mr. Oliver has created yet another intricate mystery that reads much like a good novel. It is complex with interesting twists." Hannah stopped and looked up at Martin, "But two of the reviews feel something is not quite right."

"Listen to this!" she said. "At times one feels as if the book were written for an earlier era, perhaps due to some old-fashioned language in places." The other one says, "With such complex writing Mr. Oliver can be forgiven for a few errors in the London settings he describes."

"Those are interesting comments but what I find even more interesting is that Troy can write such complex books so quickly," was Martin's reply.

"Maybe he has assistants," she answered. "Some of the big blockbuster authors only write an outline. Someone else does the first draft and then the author does the final polish."

"I doubt if Troy is in their league. In any case he certainly leads you to believe he writes everything himself," Martin answered.

"Well, I am going to start reading this tonight," she replied holding up the book she had just bought. "And I am going to look for errors. See if I can spot any words or phrases that are no longer in common use and any settings that are not quite right."

Chapter 14

The next morning, a little bleary eyed from having read late into the night, Hannah met Gemma and Trudy to complete their work. They were all anxious to finish early. The two women wanted to get to the school to receive comments from students on the changes they had made. Hannah was curious to do some follow up on what she had learned when reading Troy Oliver's book. She had not read the whole book but had read enough to make her want to search out the British Library.

They finished just past one o'clock and went their separate ways agreeing to meet the next morning to do the final edit. Hannah walked toward the Baker Street tube where she bought a sandwich and ate it while waiting for the number 30 bus that would take her to the new British Library.

Traffic was heavy as she exited the bus onto busy, noisy Euston Road. Walking toward the library she recalled that the building's architecture was not universally liked and she was a bit confused as she approached the entrance. The first possibility was through an outside coffee shop. A bit further on was the second possible entrance with little signage to announce the library. Inside the courtyard the facade of the library was not very interesting. There was, however, a stunning view of the roofs of neighboring St Pancras Station which had been recently renovated. It was an impressive Victorian pile of red brick which now served as the terminal for Eurostar. It also housed shops, bars, restaurants, and Europe's longest champagne bar.

Hannah daydreamed about the pleasant journeys to France she and Martin had taken from here on the high speed train. "It certainly is nicer than flying," she thought.

She entered the library and the inside space, unlike the outside of the building, did not disappoint. It was light, open, and airy with a soaring inner room built in the center containing precious books that could be seen through glass walls. Hannah walked up the stairs to the upper ground floor to the reader registration room. She approached a desk at the entrance where a woman with frizzy hair and glasses on the tip of her nose was working at her computer. Hannah waited a few moments and the woman looked up at her over her reading glasses.

"Yes?" she said making it a question.

Hannah explained she wanted to do some research. "I want to investigate tube stations that are no longer in use. I've learned that some were built but never used and others were used but then closed and abandoned for a variety of reasons."

"The Transport Museum would be a more appropriate place to search for that information," the woman said crisply. "We do not give access to our collection if the information one seeks is available at other locations. Also before anyone can register to get a Reader's Pass, one must search the library's online catalogues and give us specific titles of works one requires. Have you done that?"

Hannah hesitated and responded that no she hadn't looked at the online catalogues. "But I am certain you will have what I require," she added quickly.

The woman went back to her work dismissing Hannah with, "Plus it usually takes about 70 minutes to deliver items to our readers and you haven't even looked to see what you need. It is already past two o'clock. I don't think you would get much done this afternoon."

Hannah started to walk away, looked at the woman again and decided to make one last attempt.

"I know I haven't followed the steps required to get a Reader's Pass, but I am leaving London the day after tomorrow and I really would like this information. Because it is after two o'clock I don't have the time to get to the Transport Museum. Even if I get there in time I don't know if there would be someone available to help me."

The woman gave her a hard look and she knew she was about to be told to leave when Hannah quickly said, "Do you know Troy Oliver's books?"

Surprised by this out of context remark the woman replied that she did. "I find them quite intelligent and enjoyable," she answered.

Hannah attempting to find a bond with the woman said, "I recently met him in the States, had lunch with him in fact."

The woman became animated and her frizzy hair seemed to get curlier as if it has been electrified. "Oh," she breathed, "Is he as handsome as he looks on the covers of his books?"

Hannah wasn't sure what to say since she found Troy Oliver a bit smarmy. "He is very good looking if you like that type. As for me I prefer a more rugged looking man. His looks are too boyish for me, too pretty."

Before the librarian could respond Hannah said, "The reason I wanted to find out about disused tube stations is that I think he made a mistake in his last book and included a tube station that is no longer in service." She went on to tell her about the reviews she had read saying there were some errors in his London settings.

Hannah could see that this piqued the woman's curiosity. She stood up adjusting her voluminous skirt and introduced herself. "I am Fiona Hardcastle-Bottom and things like this really interest me. I especially like reading historical fiction to see that the history part is factual."

She turned to her computer typed in a few words and then said to Hannah, "I will give you a note which will allow you to use the Social Sciences Reading Room. It is on the first floor. I will see that the material you need gets to you in less than a half hour. But do come back to tell me what you found."

Fiona delivered on her promise and Hannah found herself in a cubicle with four books on London transport history. It did not take her long to find what she needed.

"Well," she said excitedly to Fiona returning to report to the woman, "Troy Oliver used the South Kentish Town tube station on the Northern Line in his latest book. But this was closed in 1924. Hardly anyone used the station because it was too close to Camden Station and Kentish Town Station. It just wasn't needed. But you can still see the platform when the train passes through."

The woman enthusiastically nodded her head. "Did you know there was a famous 1951 BBC broadcast about this station by John Betjeman? He was named our poet laureate in 1972. In addition to being a poet, he was also a writer and BBC broadcaster."

Hannah told Fiona she knew that Betjeman had been poet laureate but was unaware of his other work.

"He was a very talented man," Fiona replied. "People enjoyed listening to his BBC broadcasts. In the one about the North Kentish Town station he told the story of a Mr. Basil Green, a tax inspector who used this branch of the Northern Line daily. Like most commuters he didn't pay attention to his trip but knew his stop by instinct. One Friday the train made an unofficial stop at the closed South Kentish Town station and the doors opened. Thinking it was his stop Mr. Green stepped out on the platform. The doors closed and off went the train."

Hannah listened to the tale.

"Of course Mr. Green quickly realized his error as he stood there in the dark. He somehow found his way to the spiral staircase. You know the tubes have elevators or escalators but also staircases for emergencies. You can imagine Mr. Green's shock when after climbing the 294 stairs his head bumped against a ceiling. This was the floor of the shop that had taken over the tube station. He climbed back down and went to sleep."

"No ending was given to the story," Fiona added.

"I ran across a similar account in one of the books I was researching," Hannah announced. She took out her notes. "In my account it was a Mr. Brackett, not Mr. Greene, and he finally escaped by tearing old posters off the tube walls and setting them on fire as a train came through. The driver saw the flames and stopped." Then she added, laughing, "I also read that this tale was based on a true event. The train did stop; the doors did open, but no passenger got out."

The two women shared a few more stories about disused tube stations. Hannah said she wondered if there was one on Hampstead Heath.

Fiona told about the famous Brompton Road Station. Within a year of its opening no trains stopped there since there was no demand. However when the trains went by the guards called out 'Passing Brompton Road'. This cry became part of London's transport culture like today's 'Mind the Gap!'

"There are lots of stories like these," Fiona told Hannah. "When you return to London I will properly register you for the reading rooms and you can learn about them."

Hannah thanked the woman saying she would indeed return. Exiting the library she decided to take the nearby King's Cross tube to Kentish Town to see if she could find the disused South Kentish Town Station.

She exited the Kentish Town tube to a busy street of utilitarian shops. She knew the area since she sometimes bought fish from a fishmonger on the High Street. As she walked south, she studied buildings for any hints of former use as a station. Then suddenly there it was. It was obvious. There were the ruby-red glazed tiles and arched fan lights above the doors that were typical of many stations. It presently was being used as an upmarket pawn shop.

"Well," Hannah said to herself, "Troy Oliver certainly made a mistake when he used this for a clandestine meeting in his recent book."

She stopped at an Italian delicatessen to buy fixings for an easy dinner and was setting the table when Martin arrived. She poured two glasses of wine and they went to the terrace.

"I've been thinking about Maddie's death all day," Martin told her. "I wonder why Maddie had photos of stolen art in her house. I also wonder if the photos were of the originals or taken from the web or books?"

"Lots of things to ask about when we get back to the Cape," Hannah replied.

"What about Troy's book. Did you find the errors that the critics mentioned?"

Over dinner she told him about her trip to the British Library and the help she received from Fiona Hardcastle-Bottom. "She was a bit of a character and a big help. When we come back in the fall I plan to go to see her and get registered properly. Maybe we can even have tea together."

"I think I will read Troy's book tonight," said Martin. "By all accounts it is a page turner, but I am curious about the historical errors. Seems sloppy of Troy, especially since the book is supposed to be so well written."

Chapter 15

Martin was running on the Heath when Hannah left the flat to meet Trudy and Gemma. It was a lovely Saturday morning and she decided to walk for a while in Regent's Park. It was bustling with joggers, walkers, dog walkers. Groups of young men with their soccer kits were assembling for games. Even though Hannah enjoyed working with her friends she hated going indoors on this glorious morning.

"Good news," Gemma said as the three women settled to their work. "Our meeting with the students went very well yesterday and last night Trudy and I made the changes we thought necessary. We really only had to tweak it. So we should be able to finish in an hour or so."

They carefully reviewed the changes and in no time decided they were finished and were quite pleased with the result. "I think this is a very good program," said Trudy. "The next step is to send it to the publishing company and then wait to hear if they accept it as is or want some editing. In the meantime we can use it at the school with our students."

The friends chatted about students and the school and finally said their good-byes. "What are you and Martin doing today?" Gemma asked. "You hardly had a chance to enjoy London on this short stay."

"I am meeting Martin at the National Theatre," Hannah replied. "He planned on being there early to see if he could get tickets. The box office opens at 9:30."

"He might be lucky," said Gemma. "Last week we were able to get tickets for the Shaw play even though it is very popular. The theatre always has some tickets available for that day's performance. You have to buy them in person and you have to get in the queue early. Also, you are restricted to two tickets."

They went their separate ways, Gemma and Trudy to St John's Wood and Hannah to the Baker Street tube station where she took the Metropolitan Line to Embankment. As she walked across the pedestrian bridge over the Thames she stopped to admire some of the iconic sites of the city - the dome of St. Paul's, the new towering Shard, and the London Eye.

Martin was waiting at the entrance to the theatre waving two tickets in his hand. "I got the tickets. The matinee is at two. Let's have lunch at the Terrace Restaurant. It is such a beautiful day I want to eat outside. And it has a great view of the river."

"What a gorgeous spot!" said Hannah as they settled at their table and ordered lunch. "We have nearly 90 minutes before the play starts so we can relax and enjoy the ambiance," Martin replied proposing a toast with his glass of wine. "To a great city!"

"This short trip has been fun," Hannah said. "But I am itching to get back to Oyster Town to learn more about Maddie's death. Chief Lee will tell us about the investigation when we see her but I don't think she wants to email us any information."

"That will have to wait until we get back to the States," said Martin. "In the meantime I have more information about Troy Oliver's book." He told Hannah that when he read the book the night before he found some more discrepancies. "In the book, Troy uses the term 'sixpence' and 'shilling' and the slang term for shilling, a 'bob'. These are terms for what the English call old money. Old money was phased out after 1971 when the system changed to a decimal one with 100 pennies to the pound. The old system had 240 pennies to the pound. Troy's book is set in the present so his use of sixpence and shilling is an anachronism."

"I wonder why he made such a mistake? In the States, though, few people probably noticed," Hannah mused.

"The other discrepancy, again one Americans probably wouldn't catch, had to do with Victorian cemeteries, precisely the reason why we came on this trip. In 1800 London had a population of 1 million people. By 1850 the population had more than doubled. As you can imagine this increase in population caused all kinds of challenges for the city, not least of which was where to bury the dead. Churchyards were overcrowded. Thousands were buried in shallow pits very close, even inches, away from one another."

"I am certain that caused some health worries," Hannah interjected.

"To help alleviate the problem, investors created private cemeteries, many of which were on the fringes of the city. Some records were kept at the cemetery and some in off-site offices. These records had a variety of information such as name, age, occupation, date of death, and location of grave. The organization that hired me was given a grant to consolidate all of this and make it available on the web.

He paused and Hannah thought about the number of interesting projects Martin had been involved in over the years. "Which," Martin said awakening Hannah out of her reverie, "brings me back to Troy Oliver's book.

You remember what I said about the location of many of these cemeteries?"

"Yes," Hannah replied, "because I thought of Highgate Cemetery. When it was established Highgate was at the fringes of the city. Hampstead and Highgate were considered villages in Victorian times. Places for people to escape the city and come for fresh air."

"Right," said Martin, "and you and I have visited Highgate Cemetery a number of times. Sometimes we've brought guests to see the imposing tomb of Karl Marx and other times we just wandered through the tangle of shrubs and piles of grave stones."

"True," said Hannah, "but we haven't gone there in quite some time. Not since the Friends of Highgate Cemetery have restricted the opening times. I don't think the entrance on Chester Road, the one we used most often, is open any more. I think there is an entrance fee or at least a good will donation. We don't cross through it on a regular basis like we used to."

"Exactly," Martin nodded, "but in Troy's book Highgate Cemetery is opened all the time like it used to be, both the main gate and the gate off Chester Road by the library."

At that point Martin looked at his watch telling Hannah it was time to take their seats for the play. That evening they were busy organizing themselves for their flight back to Boston, so they did not return to the subject of Troy Oliver's books.

Chapter 16

When the Brewsters arrived back at the Cape late Sunday afternoon Hannah phoned both Jeff and Miyu to ask them to go out to dinner. She and Martin were anxious to hear any news on the investigation into Maddie's death.

"Neither one of them is answering. How frustrating! I guess we will have to wait until tomorrow to talk with them."

Martin nodded and said, "Let's just grab a light supper at The Pirates Pub and go to bed early. I am weary from the trip."

As they entered the pub they acknowledged a few people they knew. It was busy with both locals and tourists. "We might not find a table," Martin said to Hannah looking around the room. Then he saw Izzy waving to them. He was with Abby Wiley and motioned them over. "We have space in our booth," he said. "It is really crowded tonight. Why not join us."

The Brewsters accepted the invitation and Abby asked about their recent trip to London, and Izzy talked about plans Abby had for the display at the museum. "Abby was thinking that in addition to the exhibit at the museum we should put a lot of Hannah's research on the web. I am writing a grant. If the museum is awarded it would you be willing to do the work?" Izzy asked Martin.

The subject eventually turned to Maddie's death. "I heard that Maddie was seen with Gerard in his sailboat a few days before she died," Izzy told them.

The whole town apparently was abuzz speculating about what had happened.

"Chief Lee has said nothing and has issued no statements. The press simply reports that an investigation is taking place with the assistance of the state police," Izzy finished.

Their waiter, who had overheard Izzy's remarks, joined the conversation. "A friend of mine told me Maddie was sailing with Gerard. I also heard that the police want to talk to him but they can't locate him. He isn't at home and no one has seen him."

Abby waited until they had left the restaurant to take Hannah aside. "I went to Boston a few days ago to see some friends. I took the Logan bus and when I got off at South Station I realized Gerard was on the same bus. He was sitting in the back and I was in the front. I waved to him as the bus left to head for the airport, but he didn't return my wave."

"You have to tell Chief Lee about this," Hannah said emphatically. "From what we just heard in the restaurant, the police want to talk to him."

As the Brewsters drove home they discussed the situation. "This could just be town gossip," said Martin. "Gerard may or may not have been in his boat with Maddie, and there may be a perfectly logical reason why he left Oyster Town."

"Hopefully, we will get some information from Miyu in the morning," Hannah said. "I left messages for her and Jeff inviting them to breakfast tomorrow morning."

Hannah was up early and waiting impatiently for Miyu and Jeff to arrive. She made coffee and gathered the fixings for vegetable omelets. "I am anxious to hear what Chief Lee has to say," Hannah said to Martin as he filled his coffee cup. "I think we missed a lot when we were gone."

"We'll see," said Martin. "After all we were only gone a few days. And Jeff would have called us if anything really important had happened."

Minutes later Jeff arrived. They watched as he tried to close his truck door, then finally kicked it shut. "Are you going to get that door fixed?" asked his father. Jeff looked a little puzzled. "Why? It might take a minute but it always shuts."

Chief Lee pulled in the driveway a few minutes later. She was driving the patrol car and told the Brewsters she had about 30 minutes before she had to report to the station.

As Hannah cooked the omelets and made toast Miyu told them about the investigation. "I can tell you some things we've learned. None of this will be confidential in an hour. We are issuing a press release this morning."

"This is a very complex case," she began. "We just got the results of the autopsy which showed there was some water in Maddie's lungs which would be consistent with drowning."

"Does that mean an accident?" Martin asked.

"Or suicide," Miyu answered.

For a moment they were quiet, contemplating this news.

They served themselves from the counter and moved out to the deck where Miyu continued, "We haven't found any evidence that Maddie wanted to take her own life. We know she had enough money and investments to be financially solvent. The autopsy showed she was in good health and not suffering from any serious disease. We haven't found any note. Her very recent behavior does not reflect a depressed person contemplating suicide. She had a bowl of wild blueberries she had apparently picked and had the fixings in her house for a blueberry pie. Her sewing machine was set up and she was making some new curtains. She had made a note to herself to buy more feed for her horse."

"So was her death an accident? Did she fall out of a boat?" Hannah asked

"That is a possibility," Miyu answered looking at her watch. "I have to leave in a minute or two. Very quickly I can tell you that we haven't found an abandoned boat. We do though have a credible witness who saw Maddie and Gerard in his boat. But not on the day she died. We want to ask Gerard about his relationship with Maddie but we have not been able to locate him for questioning."

"I think Abby Wylie is planning on talking with you this morning," said Hannah.

"Yes," Miyu interrupted. "She has a 10 o'clock appointment. Do you know why she wants to see me?"

Hannah explained about Abby seeing Gerard on the Logan bus.

"That should be very helpful. With the careful records kept on flights and passengers nowadays it should be fairly easy to get information on Gerard and his flight." Chief Lee stood up to leave adding, "Some things won't be in the press release. Like the bruising around the carotid artery. We are very interested in this. I think you already know about the bruising. Doc said he told you about it."

"By we, Miyu means the local police and the state police. Lt. Connolly is back," Jeff told his parents.

"Does this mean late night sessions with him, pondering the case?" he teased Miyu.

She tossed her pony tail and grinned at him. "Maybe," was her reply.

She became serious again. "I said the case was complex and it is. We, yes I am including Lt Connelly," she added looking at Jeff. "We think this is a murder case but it may be hard to prove. Remember I said there was some water in Maddie's lungs." They nodded and Miyu continued. "The medical examiner believes there should have been more water."

"What do you mean?" asked Hannah.

Miyu looked her watch and started for the door. "The murderer," she replied, "was being clever. He tried to confuse things to make it look like an accident or suicide. If Maddie had been strangled to death there wouldn't have been any water in her lungs. She would have been dead when she entered the water."

Miyu paused, "The problem is there was water in her lungs but we are suspicious about the amount – very little. We think she was choked until unconscious and then thrown in the water. The bruising along the carotid artery is consistent with strangling. The autopsy showed there had been some loss of blood to the brain shortly before death. We believe she was strangled until nearly dead which is why she had some but not much water in her lungs."

She sighed. "We have to prove this. Maybe things will develop during the day. Why not come to Jeff's tonight. He is having a cookout and Lt. Connolly is invited."

"That's news to me," Jeff said to his parents as they watched the patrol car leave the driveway.

"Can you pick up some food for this cookout?" he asked his mother. "I've got to go collect the press release and then drive to P-town for a meeting with Dixie. We are planning a special midsummer supplement to the paper."

As he started his truck he added, "Better buy extra. The theatre is dark on Monday and Tuesday so Lola isn't working. When she sees cars at my house she'll be curious and will drop in. Maybe Armand too. Oh and that author wanted to see my guitars. I might call and invite him."

Martin and Jeff had a variety of food on the grill from the usual cookout fare to clams casino, shrimp and scallops. Hannah had prepared a large pot of gazpacho and a green salad. Others brought hors d'oeuvres and drinks. Ice cream was on hand for dessert.

Lola immediately attached herself to Lt. Connelly who seemed to enjoy the attention. He was still in his uniform which gave him a commanding presence among the others dressed in tee shirts and shorts. "You state policemen are so manly," she sighed, batting her eyes. "I love a man in uniform."

"Only Lola can use an old line like that and get away with it," Miyu laughed as Lola led the policeman away from the party and toward the pond.

"Let's get a glass of wine," Hannah suggested to Miyu. Just as they entered the kitchen they heard the booming voice of Gino Santos. He was boasting to Troy and Armand about the progress made in the search for Gerard. "We have a lead on Gerard. He took a US Airways flight to Plattsburg, New York, where he rented a car. That is in upstate New York on Lake Champlain, in case you don't know."

"Which Gino didn't know, by the way," Miyu whispered to Hannah.

"Time to relax and be off duty, Gino," Miyu said lightly but gave him a warning look which stopped him from giving any more information.

"Do you know if he stayed in Plattsburg?" asked Troy. Having been warned Gino was cautious and more circumspect. "Sorry guys but that's all the information I am going to give."

Troy seemed a bit disappointed and was about to ask another question when Armand said sarcastically. "I for one am glad you have this case to work on. Maybe you will leave me alone. Really Miyu I feel as if I am being harassed," he said to the police chief.

Armand sidled up next to Hannah and said quietly, "The police seem to have me under surveillance. The patrol car drives down my dirt road several times a week."

"I am sure it is your imagination," Hannah gave as a response.

He grinned, and then spoke loudly enough to include the Chief in his comments, "Or maybe they want to know why I go out in my boat at all hours."

Hannah extricated herself and poured a glass of wine for herself and Miyu. She was dying to ask about Gerard but knew she would not get any information from the police officer in so public a setting. Instead she turned to Troy Oliver and said, "Did you know that Martin and I were just in London?" He asked a few polite questions about their trip. The others had gone outside on the deck so Hannah decided it would be all right to tease Troy.

"Your book received some wonderful reviews," she told him. "And the people I talked with over there really enjoyed it. You know the comments – complex, intricate."

Troy proudly acknowledged the comments.

"But you made some mistakes," Hannah said. "Like using the terms for the old English currency and having a scene set at a tube station that is no longer in use."

His expression turned dark. "I know. I read the reviews. I'll have to be more careful in the future. But the bottom line is the critics loved the book. They have praised all my books," Troy smiled slightly. He excused himself saying he wanted to talk with Jeff about his guitars.

Hannah could not help herself and said in a slight mocking tone, "You play the guitar in addition to your other talents?"

Troy ignored her comment and picked up one of Jeff's guitars. He proceeded to play a classical Spanish piece. When he finished Hannah said, "I am sorry I was teasing you. You are quite an accomplished musician."

The party was starting to break up and there were sounds of thank you and goodbye as people gathered their belongings. Martin and Hannah were among the last to leave having helped Jeff clean up. Troy Oliver was still there and as the Brewsters left he and Jeff picked up guitars and started to jam.

"Troy is a very good musician," Hannah said to Martin as they drove home. "He played a Spanish classical piece that was very impressive."

"He is joining Jeff for a performance at the Sand Bar next week. His name should draw people. That means a bigger audience for Jeff too. A good opportunity to showcase his talent."

"Hmm," was Hannah's reply. Silently she thought, "Yes Jeff has talent, but he needs to practice more and surf less."

Chapter 17

The next day Martin was at the bank discussing various CD options with Jack Snow, the manager. As they talked in Jack's office, he seemed distracted and frequently looked out the window at the highway or turned toward the glass wall which faced into the main room of the bank. After Martin had to repeat a question for the third time, Jack shrugged his shoulders and apologized.

"I'm sorry Martin," he said. I am having trouble concentrating. I am expecting Chief Lee at any moment."

Curious, Martin asked, "Is there something wrong at the bank?"

"No! No!" was his emphatic reply. "Nothing is wrong at the bank. Please don't say that since I don't want people in town thinking we might have some kind of problem." He sighed and continued, "I may as well tell you since I already confided in you that the police are coming."

Martin waited.

"Yesterday I decided to go over bank records concerning Madeleine Cooke. You know, the woman who was found dead on an oyster grant a week or so ago. I already gave Chief Lee information about her account when I wondered if she had a safe deposit box with us."

"What did you find?" Martin asked.

"Yes, she did have a safe deposit box which according to our records hadn't been opened in years. I told the police about it and they are coming to collect it."

Martin hoped Jack would continue, but all he said was, "So there are no problems with the bank. I'm just anxious to give the contents of the safe deposit box to the police."

Just as he finished saying this Chief Lee and Patrolman Santos entered the bank. Jack waved them into his office and at the same time dismissed Martin. "Could you come back later, Martin? I will be in a better frame of mind to give you my undivided attention."

The chief acknowledged Martin but did not invite him to stay.

After completing some errands Martin decided to go to the police station. He rang the buzzer and a policewoman asked him his business. He mumbled something about a ticket and his trailer. At that moment, Lt. Connelly saw him behind the security door and motioned that he be allowed into the station. He and the state policeman went into Chief Lee's office. A safe deposit box was opened on the desk with several documents spread around it. Martin hoped that Miyu might tell him something about the documents, but when the lieutenant closed the office door he asked abruptly, "How well do you know Gerard Marceau?"

Martin explained that he was part of the regatta group. There was little interaction when racing but the group had at least one social gathering each summer and one or two meetings to discuss rules and logistics during the boating season. He stopped himself before saying that many of the other sailors thought Gerard was too aggressive when racing and that he sometimes broke the rules.

Martin wanted to bring up the topic of the safe deposit box. He was about to say that Jack Snow had told him about it when Patrolman Santos opened the door to the Chief's office. As he did so it created a draft which blew some of the papers off the desk. The police officers scrambled to collect them but not before Martin had picked up a few. As Lt. Connolly took them from him, Martin saw something that shocked him.

"Did I just see a marriage certificate?" he asked in disbelief.

Chief Lee motioned to Santos to leave and close the door. Then she turned to Martin. "What did you see?" she asked.

"It seems impossible but I thought I saw a marriage certificate for Madeleine Cooke and Gerard Marceau."

The two officers exchanged glances and the Chief shrugged. "You might as well tell him about the documents. This will be in the newspapers by tomorrow."

"Most of what we found was ordinary – some old insurance policies, her birth certificate, and her will leaving her assets, which are reasonably substantial, to animal rights' charities. The most surprising things we found were the marriage certificate and the deed," explained Connolly as he handed these two documents to Martin.

The marriage certificate clearly showed Maddie and Gerard were man and wife. The deed was to Gerard's house. It was registered in both their names.

"This, coupled with the fact that Gerard left Oyster Town, incriminates him in what I believe to be Maddie's murder," Connelly said. Martin looked at Chief Lee who nodded in agreement with the state policeman.

When Martin arrived home Hannah was ready to go sailing. "I've made sandwiches and packed some fruit," she told him as she handed him the cooler.

"It will just take me a minute to change," he replied. "And do I have some news for you!"

As they sailed out of Bog Bay into Grampus Creek, Martin told her about the contents of Maddie's safe deposit box.

Hannah was so stunned she could hardly reply. "Gerard and Maddie married!" she sputtered. "I can't believe it."

"According to the marriage certificate they were married fifteen years ago. According to Maddie's birth certificate she was born in Hoosac. You know the town. It is in the western part of the state."

"Yes I know the town." But she put it out of her mind concentrating on the news about Gerard and Maddie. "I wonder if they were divorced?" Hannah asked.

"There was no divorce certificate, but there was a deed to Gerard's house and it is in both their names."

"What did Miyu and Lt. Connolly have to say about this?" Hannah asked.

"They found it pretty incriminating especially since Gerard has left town. They are in contact with the authorities in Plattsburg and have learned that he rented a car. There is an alert out in that area of New York

State but so far no reports of anyone seeing Gerard or the car."

They continued to talk about this new information and what it meant to the case. Martin was saying he wondered why Gerard went to Plattsburg when he paused, "The wind is starting to pick up, Hannah. I think we should head for home."

They were near buoy number 10 when Martin gave the command to 'Come About'. As they did, they both heard a popping noise which startled them. Hannah looked around but Martin immediately said, "Our shroud is fraying."

Hannah looked at the shroud on the starboard side. When they had come about this shroud held all the tension from the mast. Several strands of wire had uncurled near the turnbuckle.

"Those last few strands won't hold in these winds," said Martin. He gave the command, "Come About!"

The boat was now on a port tack and the shroud on this side held all the tension.

"I am going to sail on this tack and head directly to Mayo Bluff. We can beach the boat, put in on an anchor and deal with it later," Martin said as the boat steadily moved toward shore.

Just before they reached the beach, however, the Brewsters heard the same popping sound. "The port shroud just broke," Hannah said trying to stay calm.

"Take down the sails," Martin yelled. But Hannah had foreseen this command and had already uncleated the halyard to lower the mainsail. At that moment, however, the power of the wind in the sails bent the mast and it cracked. Seconds later there was a crunch and a jolt as the boat beached itself.

"Let's get the sails down before they rip," Martin yelled. They struggled with the mainsail as it caught on the broken mast.

It took them a few minutes to notice that they were being helped.

They had landed very close to Armand's house. "I saw you were in some kind of trouble. I watched as you came about and figured you were going to beach your boat here," he explained as they studied the damage.

"The mast is a loss and things look like a mess," said Martin. "But I don't see any rips in the sails."

"You were lucky you were so close to shore when the mast broke. If you had been out in Billingsgate Bay things might have been much worse."

Martin dug out the anchor and secured the boat.

As Armand drove them home, Martin thanked the artist, "I am sure the boat will be okay, but I would appreciate it if you kept an eye on things until tomorrow. We will leave the boat on an anchor in front of your house. Around eleven tomorrow morning when the tide is in we will walk *Windswept* to the landing near you and put it on the trailer."

As they sipped a glass of wine before dinner, Hannah asked, "Would we have been in serious trouble if we were far out in Billingsgate Bay when the mast broke? Armand seemed to think so."

"It would have been more of a struggle getting the sails down, and we probably would have torn the mainsail," Martin replied. "But I would have started the motor, and we would have made it back slowly but surely."

"What if we didn't have a motor?" Hannah asked. The Brewsters had a small four horse power motor on the boat. None of the other sailors who raced had motors because of the extra weight but Martin liked it as much for convenience as for safety. He often said that if the winds didn't cooperate while they were sailing – got too high or too low – he could motor back to his mooring. When they were younger they had experienced a number of adventures such as rowing back to the mooring when winds died and the tide was flowing out, or leaving their boat on an anchor off Lieutenant Island and walking across the flats to their home.

"It is a moot point since we have a motor. I have little nostalgia for the old days when we rowed or walked home." Then answering her question he said, "But today if we hadn't had a motor we would have rowed back. It would have been slow going. Or maybe a motor boat would have offered us a tow. In any case we were not in any real danger."

Chapter 18

"I heard you had a little problem yesterday," Ben said to Hannah as she opened the slider and invited him into the house. "Coffee?" she asked. He accepted a cup. "I'll help Martin secure the boat and then haul it out of the water and get it back here."

Martin was gathering cords and rope that he knew he would need to tie the mast to the boat to transport it home. "Do you think we will need to cut the mast? It wasn't completely severed. I better get a hacksaw."

Ben noticed that one of Martin's trailer tires was low. "We'll have to stop at the gas station to fill that tire," he said as they connected the trailer to Ben's truck.

Martin sighed and said to Hannah, "I hope the police are all busy with Maddie's murder. I never got around to registering the boat trailer. If any member of the police force sees me I know I will get fined."

After the two men left Hannah tended to her vegetable garden. She gave it a thorough watering, then jumped in the MG. She stopped at the post office to collect mail, and drove to Armand's house.

"I hope Ben and Martin are already there," she said to herself. "I don't want to be alone with Armand. He was helpful yesterday but when he is alone with me he is creepy."

To Hannah's relief Ben's truck was parked behind Armand's house, and she could see the two men standing by the boat. They were busy disentangling shroud and stay wires. Hannah used WD-40 to help her loosen one of the pins and then waited to see what the two men had decided to do about the broken mast. It was agreed that the three of them could lift it out of the deck and then Martin would saw it into two pieces where it was broken. After that they would secure both pieces to the cabin of the boat and bring everything home.

While Martin was busy with the hacksaw, Ben was examining the shrouds. "You know Martin," he said. "I had a funny feeling about what happened to you. What are the chances of two shrouds breaking at the same time?"

Martin stopped sawing and looked at Ben.

"It seems to me that these shrouds didn't fray. These were cut. Look how even the wires are at the break. Both shrouds look this way. Fraying is different, more irregular."

"Who would want to cut the shrouds? And why?" Martin asked incredulously while Hannah studied the wires.

"The strands are pretty even," she said to Martin.

In response to Martin's questions Ben shrugged his shoulders and said, "I don't know who or why, but maybe someone wanted to hurt you and Hannah or maybe it was some kind of practical joke."

"If someone wanted to hurt us we wouldn't have been hurt, even if we were out in Billingsgate Bay," Hannah said. "Martin told me we would have safely gotten back to our mooring. The boat might have had more damage, but we would have been okay."

"True," said Ben, "but there was the possibility of the mast falling on you."

"Not likely, though," added Martin.

"But maybe the perpetrator didn't know this. To someone who doesn't know sailboats the idea of shrouds breaking and a mast possibly breaking and falling seems pretty drastic. I bet if you asked non-sailors about this, most would think you would have been in serious trouble."

"Armand thought so," Hannah replied.

Ben studied the shrouds again and said, "I think I will ask around to see if anyone saw suspicious activity near your boat."

Martin was about to answer when Lola and Armand approached.

"Lola has a story for you," Armand said grinning.

Lola scarcely gave the damaged boat a glance. "I need help and advice," she said breathlessly, leaning slightly against Ben and looking piteously at him.

Ben moved away from Lola as she continued, "I am positive that Brocton stole a valuable antique mirror that was in Lydia's collection. He offered to help me clean the basement to give Armand some storage." She turned to Ben and explained, "Armand is going to rent gallery space from me. He did not want to have his art work displayed alongside the second rate art that Brocton just introduced to his gallery. Anyway, Armand needed storage space and Brocton offered to help. Now I know why. He wanted to get his hands on that mirror."

She grew more animated and stomped her feet. "Remember, Hannah, how he left me in the lurch. All the stuff that was spread on my lawn. Jeff and his friends had to put it back in the basement."

Hannah nodded as Lola wailed, "He is a thief!"

"Your basement is very full," Hannah said calmly. "How do you know that the mirror was stolen?

It could be in your basement behind some furniture."

Lola, however, had convinced herself that Brocton had stolen the mirror and she could not be persuaded otherwise.

"I have to get back into his basement and have a good look," she announced.

"Get back into the basement?" Hannah asked. "What do you mean by 'back'?"

"When Brocton left the gallery yesterday, I tried to search his basement. He has lots of stuff stored in it most of it boxed or wrapped. I only stayed a few minutes because I was afraid he would return."

"How did you get into the basement?" Ben asked. "Did Brocton leave the gallery unlocked?"

"I have a key," Lola said triumphantly. "I got it from Armand."

The group turned and focused on Armand. "Okay, big deal. I have a key to Brocton's gallery. He gave it to me when I was setting up one of my shows a few years ago. He forgot to ask for it back and I forgot to give it back."

"And you gave it to Lola," Hannah said shaking her head in disbelief.

"Look, Lola was quite upset and emotional about this mirror. I figured it would calm her down if she had the chance to check Brocton's basement," Armand answered.

"Armand is such a love," Lola purred. "He is always willing to help me. But now I need more advice," she said looking at each of them. "How can I spend more time in his basement so I can really do a search?" she asked.

"We have a boat to take care of," was Ben's curt reply and he and Martin went about the business of the mast. Lola continued to plead with them but to no avail. Once the boat was ready Hannah and Martin started to walk it to the nearby landing.

As Ben left to get his truck and meet the Brewsters, he said to Lola, "Be careful talking about your escapade in Brocton's basement. This is a small town. It might get back to him. He probably would press charges."

That afternoon Martin searched the internet and made phone calls getting information about repairing the fiberglass on their boat and replacing the mast.

"Hannah,'" he said to his wife. "The best place to replace the mast is in Wareham. It is the same place we went when we had our mast broken during Hurricane Bob."

Martin recalled how all the boats at the point were damaged in some way by that hurricane. "If that storm had hit during high tide when the boats had water under them I am convinced the damage would have been slight, if any. But it hit at low tide and the wind caught the masts and flipped the boats over. Doc's mast was drilled 18 feet into the sand and is still there."

"As for our present problem, I called Wareham and it will probably take weeks to get a replacement. In the meantime, I will bring *Windswept* to the boatyard in Orleans. Tony said he could make the repairs to the deck in a few days. The bad news is we will be without a boat for a while."

"I think we should bring the cut shrouds to the police station," he continued. "I can't believe anyone wanted to harm us, but if someone is playing practical jokes or going around vandalizing boats, Chief Lee should know about it."

Chief Lee was not at the station so Martin and Hannah told their story to a young officer who was filling in during the summer months. He carefully recorded what they had to say then looked at the shrouds.

"These do look cut," he agreed. "My dad owns a boat yard in Marion and I work there a lot. I have seen frayed shrouds and they don't look like this. I have replaced shrouds and cut them to fit and this is what they look like."

That evening Jeff had arranged for Troy Oliver to perform with him at the Sand Bar. "We practiced a bit the other day and I think we can pull this off," Jeff had explained to his parents.

Jeff and Troy were just finishing a set when the Brewsters were ushered to a table after waiting nearly a half hour. Hannah looked around at the unusually large crowd. "Just as I thought, Troy's name is a big draw. Jeff sometimes fills the place but tonight it is really crowded."

"Jeff and Troy are a big hit," said Miyu coming over to their table. "Troy likes the limelight, but he can really play the guitar. And Jeff knows how to improvise. They are finishing up after the next set," she told them. "The Crab Fiddlers are the next act and will play until closing. Why not come over to Jeff's when he finishes. I know he is going to be keyed up after this performance."

After Jeff and Troy finished playing, the Brewsters stayed a while listening to the bluegrass music of the Crab Fiddlers before going to Jeff's. Troy was there and Hannah and Martin complimented him on his performance. He seemed genuinely pleased by their comments.

As Martin headed to the kitchen to get himself a beer, Hannah asked Troy where he learned to play the guitar. She recalled that Jeff's formal guitar lessons started in London when a stranger rang their door bell and said he often walked by their flat and heard Jeff playing. He thought he had talent but needed lessons. The young man was a bit scruffy yet something about him convinced Martin to invite him in. He proved to be an excellent teacher and Jeff progressed steadily under his tutelage.

"I took lessons when I was a kid in my hometown," Troy responded. "But when I was around ten my mother arranged for me to take lessons from a music professor at Williams College. He happened to be a fairly well known flamenco guitarist. He usually didn't take private pupils but after I auditioned he accepted me. I worked with him for about three years. He was a great teacher."

"Well you certainly can play," said Hannah.

Jeff walked Troy to his car and when he returned he was beaming. "What a night!" he enthused. They gathered on the deck overlooking the pond. "We were a big hit! I wonder if Troy wants to do it again. If so we probably should develop a practice schedule."

They let him talk about the night's performance, the crowds, the music. Finally just as the Brewsters were getting ready to leave, Miyu said, "We are announcing at a press conference tomorrow morning that traces of Maddie's DNA were found in Gerard's boat. We can't be sure when it got there but it is incriminating especially since Gerard has left town."

When asked, Miyu told them that there were still no leads to his whereabouts. "It seems strange that no one has seen him or the rental car in the Plattsburg area. Wherever he is, he has to go out sometime to buy food."

On the way home Hannah said to Martin, "Do you realize that both Maddie and Troy come from Western Massachusetts?"

"Seems like quite a coincidence," Martin said. Then he asked, "How do you know that?"

Hannah replied, "We know Maddie was born in Hoosac, and Troy told me that as a kid he took music lessons from a professor at Williams College. That college is only a few miles from Hoosac."

Chapter 19

"What are you doing up so early?" Martin asked as he joined Hannah in the kitchen.

"We are going to Hoosac. We always enjoy going to the Berkshires," was Hannah's reply.

Martin looked doubtful and started to protest. "And we can take the bikes," Hannah quickly added. "We've wanted to ride the bike trail there. Some biking guides say it is the nicest in the state. It goes along rivers, Cheshire Lake, fresh water marshes, and old factories."

Martin still didn't look convinced. "We can see your godmother in Northampton. It has been a while since we've seen her." As she suspected this appealed to him. He was close to his godmother and enjoyed visiting her.

"Okay," Martin conceded. "But I thought we were going to go to the Berkshires in the fall before returning to London."

"We will," said Hannah. "And we will spend a few days. Maybe hike Mount Greylock. We could go for the annual ramble. But I want to go to Hoosac now because I want to ask around about Maddie and maybe Troy."

"I'll look on the web for a place to stay," Martin said finishing his coffee and heading toward his office.

"I did that last night," said Hannah. "When we leave Hoosac we will go to Northampton and stay at the Hotel Northampton. We can have dinner there at the Wiggins Tavern.

They packed quickly and Martin mounted the bikes on the Volvo. Before noon they were in the Berkshires at the southern end of the Ashuwillticook bike trail.

"The trail is eleven miles long," said Martin. "Like our bike trail on the Cape it was a former railroad route so it is flat. Do you want to see if there is a place near the trail to get a sandwich or wait until we get to Hoosac to have lunch?"

They agreed that it would probably take an hour or so to get to the end of the trail. "Let's wait," said Hannah. "We have to figure some way to get people to talk about Maddie and Troy. In a small town like Hoosac we might get lucky at a local restaurant. We can always start by talking about the old days of high school sports. Didn't we play basketball against Hoosac once when we were in high school?"

"We did," Martin replied. "Hoosac wasn't in our division, but teams from other divisions liked to play them because they were known for their good basketball teams."

"Let's try to remember a few names from the Hoosac teams," Hannah said. "Everyone, even I, used to know all the good players from western Massachusetts. That may start a conversation. Who knows? Someone might remember what a good basketball player you were."

"You knew the players because we were dating and you wanted to make a good impression on me," Martin teased. "I thought you liked basketball so I took you to college games and semi-pro games."

"And I was totally bored!"

"But you got your man!" Martin said.

Hannah grinned. "Well I haven't gone to a basketball game in years and years. Had enough when I was dating you to last a lifetime!"

They adjusted their helmets and started biking. Along the way they stopped at a panel describing the history of the trail.

"It is called the "Ashuwillticook Trail which is a Native American term meaning the pleasant river between the hills," Hannah read.

"The trail goes through the Hoosac Valley between the Hoosac mountain range and Mount Greylock," Martin said.

"And look!" he added as they emerged from a small woods. Cheshire Lake was in front of them and above was Mount Greylock, the highest elevation in Massachusetts.

"What a beautiful spot," Hannah enthused. "Greylock looks so majestic and the mountain is reflected in the water."

They biked along the lake and along wetlands until they reached a small settlement where they stopped briefly. A panel here explained that this had been a stop on the Underground Railroad. It had been a harbor for runaway slaves before the Civil War.

They continued biking going past small abandoned mills until arriving at the end of the trail in Hoosac. At the terminus was an information center where they asked about a place to have lunch.

"What do you think?" asked Martin as they left thanking the man at the desk for his help. "Do you want to try the diner, or the Mexican restaurant in the former fire station, or the oldest restaurant in the area?"

"We can decide when we see them," was Hannah's reply.

They locked their bikes and walked up Main Street. In the middle of a square was a statue of a prosperous looking man which one arm outstretched.

"That is President McKinley. The date on the statue shows it was put up after his assassination," Martin said.

"I am not surprised that the town fathers honored him," said Hannah. "The economy of all of northern Berkshire from the late 19th to the middle of the 20th century was based on manufacturing, mainly textiles. I bet the mill owners appreciated McKinley's support for business. His administration supported very high tariffs to protect American manufacturing."

"And I bet he didn't like anti-trust laws or any kind of union activities. I wonder what the mill workers thought of a statue honoring him being put in the center of their town," Martin said.

They continued up Main Street lined with Victorian buildings. "Here is one of the restaurants that was recommended for lunch," said Martin. "What do you think?"

Hannah looked in the large windows and saw a combination of booths and tables and nearly all were full. "Let's eat here," Hannah responded. "It looks promising."

A friendly hostess led them to a booth and gave them menus. The restaurant was buzzing with conversation. People were not just talking with those at their table but with people at other tables as well.

"It looks like everyone knows everyone else," said Hannah as she picked up the menu.

"And we are in luck," said Martin. "Look at the walls."

Hannah looked around her and saw that the walls were covered with photos. She asked the waitress about them when she came to take their order.

"We have a great collection of photos of local people. Some are old and some are recent. Our customers are mainly from this area and they love looking at them," was her response.

While waiting for their lunch Martin wandered around the restaurant looking at the photos. At one booth he sat down and became engaged in an animated conversation with two men. He motioned to Hannah to come over. He caught the waitress's attention and told her they would be joining the two men at their table for lunch.

Martin introduced Hannah to the two men and said, "They remember when our high school played basketball against Hoosac."

"My brother was on the team, Stan Kowalski. He was a forward. I remember that you scored over 20 points that night but we still beat your team," he said addressing his comments to Martin. " There is a picture of that Hoosac team over there on the wall."

Martin got up to look at the photo. He remembered the game but in honesty did not remember any of the faces on the team. However, framed below the photo was a book jacket from one of Troy Oliver's books.

Martin made pleasant conversation about sports in the old days and some of the winning teams and great players from western Massachusetts. Then he changed the subject. "I noticed that you have a framed book jacket from one of Troy Oliver's books. We just met him. He lives in the same town we do on the Cape. Is he from Hoosac?"

The waitress was serving them their orders and overheard Martin's question. "I grew up in the same neighborhood as Troy Oliver. He was born here but when he reached junior high age his mother, who was a widow, sent him to private school. Her father had left her some money and she decided to send him to a boarding school near Boston. So, yes, this is his hometown but he didn't have the same home town experiences as those of us who went to high school here."

"There were a few others who went to boarding school," remarked one of the men. "Mostly doctor's kids. But I think they missed out on a great experience. This was a wonderful place to be a teenager."

"Remember the church dances on Saturday nights? Going parking with your girlfriend on West Road? Getting home late and telling your parents you went to the Blue Saucer for a hamburger? We used to say everyone was there, but of course no one was since we were all parking on West Road. And then there was The Crest where a coke cost a nickel and you spent hours there listening to the juke box."

They paused, and then continued to reminisce. "How about the time we smuggled the motor scooters into the boys' room at the high school? Or getting caught smoking in the boiler room?"

Hannah tried to turn the conversation back to Troy Oliver, but it was obvious that they had no interest in him. She sighed saying to herself that they obviously hadn't really known him since he left town in his early teens.

Before leaving the restaurant Hannah decided to ask the waitress about Maddie. "Did you also know a woman named Madeleine Cooke who I think came from this town?"

The waitress became guarded. "Are you talking about the woman who was murdered recently on Cape Cod?"

Hannah nodded.

The waitress hesitated then said, "You are not from the press or one of those sensational magazines?" she asked.

"No. We live in the town where she was murdered and I knew her somewhat. We are a little curious about her marriage to a Gerard Marceau."

"I am really busy with the lunch crowd," she said. "But maybe Rose can help you." The waitress pointed to a woman sitting by herself at a table near the window. "I'll introduce you."

The Brewsters settled themselves at the table. Rose explained that she was a former high school English teacher and knew Madeleine when she was a teenager. "I never knew her husband. She married him after she left Hoosac. I overheard you also asking about Troy Oliver. I didn't know Mr. Oliver since he didn't go to the local high school. When he was thirteen, he left for boarding school."

She paused for a moment. "It is a real coincidence that Madeleine and Troy lived in the same neighborhood here and ended up in the same town on the Cape. Madeleine used to baby sit for Troy. His mother was the town librarian and Madeleine watched him after school until the library closed. His mother was a real literary type. She used to write beautiful articles that were published every month or so in the local newspaper. Once in a while she wrote short stories. Probably where Troy got his talent."

"Where in Hoosac did Troy and Madeleine live?" Martin asked.

"They lived in the neighborhood behind the library," was her reply. "I'm not certain what street. I hate to be talking about this since the whole town is worried it will be inundated by the press because of her murder."

"At the moment the media is stationed in our town on the Cape, hoping to get information from our police chief. But you are right. Once they learn that Madeleine was from Hoosac, some will come to look for a story," Martin replied and then thanked Rose for having talked with them.

They started for the door when the waitress called to them, "The lunch crowd is thinning so I have a minute to talk. Madeleine and Troy both lived near me. Madeleine was older and Troy about my age but I never really knew him. I never met Madeleine's husband. But in the summer when I was a kid, my family used to go to her family's cabin in Plainfield. It was and I imagine still is very remote. It was a simple place. All the kids bunked in the huge attic. We had fun swimming and canoeing in the small pond and exploring the woods."

"Where in Plainfield was this camp?" Hannah asked trying not to show too much curiosity?

"You know I am not certain I could find it today. I think we turned off the main road at the beginning of the pond and took the first or second right. In any case the camp was down a dirt road and was right on the pond, she said. Then she added wistfully, "Those were great summers."

The Brewsters said their goodbyes and an excited Hannah nearly ran back to their bikes.

"Whoa," said Martin. "What's your rush?"

"Martin, don't you see? Gerard must be at the cabin in Plainfield."

"But he flew to Plattsburg, New York. That is a few hundred miles north of here."

"True," said Hannah as she got on her bike. "But no one has seen him there despite the fact that the New York state police have been actively looking for him. I think Gerard flew to Plattsburg as a ruse. Right after he got there he rented a car and drove to Plainfield. He is hiding out at Maddie's cabin."

Martin didn't reply. He and Hannah biked steadily back to their car. When they arrived at the end of the trail, Martin said, "You know Hannah. I have been mulling this all over and I think you might be right about Gerard. At least it is worth looking into. But we should call Miyu."

"No, not yet," she replied. "Let's go do a little snooping before we get her involved. If we tell her our suspicions what is she supposed to do? We have to have more for her to go on."

They secured their bikes and Martin consulted a map. "We have to drive back toward Hoosac to pick up Route 116 which will take us to Plainfield," Martin reported. "But it is in the direction of Northampton so not out of our way."

Route 116 took them through a hilly, rural environment. They passed a few small dairy farms but most of the land was forested. It was scenic and felt quite remote. The mountain range they passed through isolated the northern Berkshire towns from the more prosperous bustling towns in the Connecticut River Valley. Martin drove slowly once they passed the marker indicating they had entered Plainfield.

"Look!" said Hannah. "There is an old sign for a pond. Turn here."

Martin did so and they drove down a steep hill which led to a small, nearly round body of water. It was fringed on one side with a number of small cabins.

"This doesn't feel right," said Martin. "I thought Plainfield Pond was on, not off Route 116. Also there seems to be only one road here and that skirts the pond and leads to each cabin. It isn't remote enough."

Hannah agreed and they drove back up the hill and continued east on the highway. Shortly they came upon another pond. A few cars were parked on the side of the road at a tiny beach. Except for this small sandy area the rest of the pond was surrounded by mature trees, mostly pines and dense undergrowth. Just before the beach a dirt road led into these woods.

"This is more like it," said Hannah, as they took a left.

They came upon a fork in the road and Martin turned right toward the pond. Immediately in front of them was a well maintained camp with freshly painted dark green shutters.

"This place is visible from Route 116 and the small beach where those families are swimming," said Martin. "I don't think this is the place. I'm going to take the left fork. I think it continues around the pond."

The road became very bumpy and overgrown with bushes that scraped against the sides of their car. Ahead was what appeared to be a rough driveway.

"That looks like it might lead to a cabin," said Martin. As they drove further they could make out a roof line among the trees.

"Stop the car," said Hannah. "I want to explore on foot. If we drive down we might be seen."

Martin told her he was going to turn the car around to get it in a position to drive out quickly if necessary. "Be careful, Hannah," he cautioned. "Don't get too close to the house. Promise!"

Hannah nodded and started down the dirt road toward the pond and the cabin. As she got closer to the building she saw a car partially covered by a tarp. There was a bit of open land for a picnic table and what looked like a fire pit, but most of the land was heavily vegetated with trees and bushes. Hannah used these to stay hidden from anyone who might be watching from the cabin. As she got closer to the car, she paused, listening carefully for any sounds. Hearing nothing she got on all fours and crawled to the car and lifted the tarp. The car had New York license plates.

Hannah wanted to run back to Martin but she forced herself to retreat slowly and carefully. When she was at the end of the driveway she raced down the road to the car.

"Martin," she gasped. "I think we found Gerard!"

Frustratingly the Brewsters had to drive a few miles before they got a signal on their cell phone. Martin then called Chief Lee to report what they had discovered. He also gave the license number of the car which Hannah had memorized.

"I'll call the state police in Northampton. Plainfield is in their district," Chief Lee said. "Wait for them on the road. Don't go back to the cabin!"

They drove back to Plainfield Pond and waited. It seemed like hours but was probably no more than forty minutes when two patrol cars arrived.

The police were well informed about Gerard, his flight to Plattsburg, and Maddie's murder.

"The license matches the car that Mr. Marceau rented in Plattsburg," one of the officers told them. "We are going to arrest him."

By that time two more police vehicles had arrived. It was obvious that the authorities were taking this seriously. They told the families who had been enjoying a day of swimming to leave the beach and told Martin and Hannah to stay in their car.

"You were right, Hannah. Gerard tried to fool everyone by flying to New York and then driving here where he could hide out."

"Poor, Gerard," answered Hannah. "I can't believe he is a murderer."

Just then a cavalcade of police vehicles exited the dirt road. They could just glimpse Gerard in the back of one of them.

An officer approached their car and said, "We have him in custody. He gave up very easily. Claims he is innocent. We would like you to stop at the barracks in Northampton to give a statement."

Chapter 20

The Brewsters awoke after a troubled sleep. Through the night both of them thought of Gerard. He was the topic of their conversation at breakfast. The visit with Martin's godmother proved to be a good distraction for them and after promising to visit again, "Probably this fall," Martin said, they headed back to the Cape, arriving home late afternoon.

While Martin unpacked the car, Hannah jumped into the MG and drove to town to get a few groceries. As she entered the deli she nearly bumped into Troy Oliver.

"I was just in your hometown," Hannah said with a smile.

"I know," he replied. "News travels quickly in Oyster Town. Everyone is talking about how you and Martin helped arrest Gerard."

"We found out where he was hiding," she responded. "And the state police from Northampton made the arrest."

"So is he being charged with Maddie's murder? Is the investigation over?" Troy asked. "Everyone is curious."

"I'm not sure," answered Hannah. "The last time we saw Gerard he was in the back seat of a state police vehicle. I haven't seen Chief Lee since our return. Even if I did she becomes very tight lipped when Lt. Connolly is around." She paused and then sighed, "But, you know, it is hard to believe Gerard killed Maddie."

She then changed the subject. "A lot of people in Hoosac remembered Maddie and they remembered you, too, even though you didn't go to high school there. We talked with some folks who knew your mother. They told us she was the librarian and also a good writer. She wrote articles for the newspaper but also wrote some short stories. Did you get your talent from her? Or any ideas?"

Troy shifted his load of groceries and looked puzzled? "Did anyone say I got my ideas from my mother? That isn't true. Please don't go around town saying this. You know how people love to gossip and there are a number of professors from my university who spend part of the summer here in Oyster Town. Some are jealous of me and would be happy to spread false stories."

Hannah was about to ask him about having Maddie as a neighbor in Hoosac, when she realized they were blocking the entrance and getting nasty looks from other customers. Hannah apologized to them, waved good-bye to Troy, and headed to the deli counter.

She returned home and found a note from Martin. He was at the Wequassett Inn. A company with which he had an on-going contract was having a small conference on the Cape and he was asked to meet with a few of the company's directors for drinks, dinner, and a little business.

"He will have a nice dinner overlooking Pleasant Bay," thought Hannah. Not sure what she now wanted to do for dinner, she organized her purchases and drove to Jeff's. She prepared some skewers of swordfish, onion, mushrooms, and green peppers and made a Greek salad.

"If Jeff comes home we can have dinner together. If not I can grill the shish-ka-bobs and leave him leftovers," she thought.

She was about to change into her bathing suit for a swim when she heard Lola call her name.

"I saw your car," Lola explained, as she walked in and made herself at home on Jeff's couch.

They talked a bit but Lola seemed unusually distracted.

"You have something on your mind, don't you?" Hannah asked.

Lola hesitated and then said, "This morning I was at the library and I heard Brocton tell Cindy that he was going to Boston for a few days to an art sale."

"So?" asked Hannah.

"So," replied Lola, "I want to go into the basement of Brocton's art gallery again to see if he put the antique mirror there."

Hannah stared at her. "You want to do what?"

Lola continued hurriedly, "I want to get into the basement of his gallery. We can do it together. I am afraid to do it myself."

"This is a crazy idea," Hannah replied.

"Remember, I have the key. Armand gave it to me," Lola smiled and dug into the pocket of her skin tight jeans and pulled out a key. "We can go in, check the basement, and leave without anyone knowing."

Hannah refused to be a part of Lola's plan and said she was going to take a swim.

"Hannah," Lola pleaded. "I am going to search Brocton's basement whether you come with me or not. Please come with me. I'll get you free tickets to every play at the theater for the rest of the summer."

Hannah started to relent thinking that they could be in and out of the basement in just a few minutes.

"Forget the tickets," she told Lola. "I'll come with you, but if we don't find anything in a few minutes we are leaving, agreed?"

"I am so relieved," Lola said breathlessly. "Let's go!"

The two women walked up the dirt road and turned toward Brocton's gallery. "The key is for the back door," explained Lola as she quickly walked down the shell driveway to the small backyard. Here she let out a sigh of relief. "I don't think anyone saw us," she said.

She slid the key in the lock and slipped inside. "Brocton's gallery is nearly a twin of Lydia's place," said Lola. "The basement door is this one."

"I know it is a twin of Lydia's," answered Hannah. "From my research I learned they were attached buildings when they were on Billingsgate and continued to be joined when they were floated to Oyster Town. Brocton moved his section several years ago. He owned the land across from Lydia's antique shop, and he thought it would be better for his business to be a separate independent building."

The two women descended the steep, narrow stairs. There was just enough light from the two basement windows for them to see clearly.

"Brocton keeps a tidy basement," Hannah said, thinking of the collection of tools, paints, gardening equipment and whatnot that accumulated so quickly in the Brewster basement.

At first glance they saw there was an assortment of items all neatly boxed or in bundles, four small file cabinets, along with various equipment for hanging or otherwise displaying paintings and sculpture.

"I don't see anything that looks like a mirror," Hannah said. "Let's go."

"What about those packages over there," Lola said too stubborn to give up just yet.

Hannah felt the bundles which were wrapped in blankets and turned to Lola. "These feel like canvasses, probably paintings. There is no mirror inside. Come on Lola. We have to go."

Reluctantly Lola agreed. "Brocton must have my mirror at his house or maybe he took it off Cape to sell."

Hannah ignored the young woman thinking she was becoming obsessed by this mirror. At the top of the stairs she turned the handle of the door only to find it would not open. She tried to remain calm and turned it once again. Nothing.

"Lola," she said looking over her shoulder at the blonde, "I think we are locked in."

Lola pushed Hannah aside and twisted the door handle. When the door didn't open she banged on it and pushed it with her shoulder. Then she sunk to the stairs and started to cry.

Hannah closed her eyes trying to concentrate. "No use blaming Lola for this situation," she said to herself. "I agreed of my own free will to come with her."

"Calm down, Lola. Let's try to think of something we can do to get out of here."

They returned to the basement. Hannah looked at the windows. They were high on the wall. "Even if we find something to stand on to reach the windows we would never get out," Hannah said. "This building is old and these basement windows are tiny."

"I've got it!" Lola said. "I have my cell phone. We can call Martin or Jeff."

"Not Martin!" said Hannah quickly not wanting to think about his reaction to their predicament. "He is in Harwich. Let's call Jeff."

Lola dug in her back pocket for the phone, looked at it and started to cry again. "There is no signal," she wailed.

Slowly the reality of their situation sunk in and Hannah felt like joining her in a good cry.

"I'm hungry," Lola moaned. "No one knows where we are. Brocton is going to be away for a few days. We may be stuck here. How long can someone live without food and water?"

"We are not going to die here," Hannah responded trying not to get angry. "We need to be rational," she said to Lola. "Let's think!"

Time passed as they sat in silence and the room grew dark.

"Lola," Hannah said breaking the silence. "I have a solution but it will end up with us getting in trouble over this whole episode. Maybe even arrested."

Lola reached out to take her hand. "Let's just get out of here. I don't care what happens."

"Okay. We have to put on the basement lights. Find something we can break a window with and start hollering, maybe a passerby or someone from the Bayberry Inn across the road will hear us."

Lola found some wire clippers and started to throw them at the window. On her third attempt the window crashed. "We are lucky this is old glass. It shattered easily. Now we start to shout," ordered Hannah.

A Cape Cod Mystery

The two women pulled the canvasses which were wrapped in old blankets near the window. Then they sat down and took turns calling for help.

It was getting darker and darker outside and they were getting hoarse.

"Let's stop for a bit," pleaded Lola. "I can't ruin my voice. I am an actress and I need it for the play."

"Now that it is dark, maybe someone will notice the light on in the basement and report it," was Hannah's answer.

Hannah was bored and to pass the time she unrolled the blankets from one of the wrapped canvases they had been sitting on. "You see," said Hannah as the wrappings fell away. "I was right. These are paintings not your mirror."

Then two things happened. She unrolled the canvas to look at the painting and what she saw stunned her. She was positive it was one of the stolen paintings she had discussed with Trudy and Gemma. And Maddie had had a photograph of it. At nearly the same moment the basement door opened and a voice called, "This is the police!"

Lola ran up the stairs crying hysterically giving Hannah a few minutes to think and act. She quickly wrapped the painting around her waist and threw the blanket over herself just as the two police officers disentangled themselves from Lola and came down the stairs.

Hannah did not recognize either of the two officers. She let Lola try to explain the situation knowing that she would just exasperate them.

It quickly became clear that the police were going to bring them to the station where they would most likely be charged with breaking and entering.

When one of the officers ordered Hannah up the stairs her only reply was that she was very cold, probably from shock. Could she keep the blanket around her? Then she asked, "How did we get locked in?"

The officer looked at the door handle. "You were unlucky," was his reply. "This basement door has an old locking device. When it is unlocked it is vertical and when locked horizontal. I think when you closed the door behind you the lock fell into the horizontal, locked position."

Just as they were getting into the patrol car Lola again went into hysterics, pleading with the officers who weren't certain what to do with this attractive young woman in her rather tight jeans.

Hannah took advantage of this diversion and the darkness to pull the painting from around her waist and drop it behind some bushes. "When I get out of this situation, if I get out of it," she said to herself, "I will come back to get the painting."

A surprised looking Chief Lee was at the station when they stumbled in, Lola continuing to protest. After several attempts to get the story straight, Chief Lee looked sternly at both women. "I am going to release you on personal recognizance but I am also going to charge you for breaking and entering."

Things only got worse for Hannah as she faced Martin to tell him what she and Lola had done. It was a quiet ride as Martin drove Lola to her apartment and then headed home. "I will call a lawyer in the morning. I think you will need one," he said as Hannah went off to bed.

Chapter 21

Hannah awoke early and went for a run. She extended it by a few miles since she dreaded facing Martin at what she expected would be a tense atmosphere at breakfast. She felt guilty about breaking into Brocton's basement with Lola, but at the same time felt elated about finding the painting and anxious to retrieve it as soon as possible that morning.

When she returned home she heard Martin in his office talking on the phone. She couldn't hear the conversation but did hear him laugh loudly. When she had showered and was setting the table for breakfast Martin gave her a hug from behind. Surprised that he wasn't angry she turned toward him.

"I just got off the phone with my lawyer friend, Peter Van Kamp, and he thought your situation was quite funny and I suppose he made me see the humorous side of it. The two of you by accident getting locked in Brocton's basement. I can imagine Lola got pretty hysterical."

"She did at times," Hannah answered. "What did Peter say would happen to me?" she asked cautiously.

"As soon as Chief Lee makes a formal charge, he will come down from Boston to review the case with her. He will then talk with you and Lola," Martin paused. "We might as well have him represent Lola as well since you are both charged with the same crime."

"Crime," Hannah repeated, "that sounds awfully serious."

"Peter said it can be serious but he also thinks that everything can be settled out of court, especially if Brocton is cooperative."

"Yes but will he cooperate?" Hannah mused.

She was silently wondering what excuse to give in order to leave the house and retrieve the painting when Martin solved her dilemma.

"Hannah, I arranged for a meeting this morning with one of the company representatives I had lunch with yesterday. We need to clear up a few points. I should be back by the afternoon. Maybe we can go kayaking? We could go from Mayo Beach and skirt Great Island. The weather is nice and winds are light and in the afternoon the tide will be rising. The return trip will be easy since we will be going with the tide."

Hannah quickly agreed, anxious to have Martin leave.

Moments after he left Hannah headed to Jeff's house. She was lucky again since Jeff wasn't at home. She parked her car and walked up the dirt road, passing Lola's apartment in the former antique shop and crossing toward Brocton's gallery. In case anyone observed her, she tried to look nonchalant as she walked down his driveway. When she was behind the building she quickly rustled through the bushes finding the hidden painting. She retrieved it and carefully rolled the canvas.

As she retraced her steps back to Jeff's, one or two cars passed her. They had out of state license plates so Hannah knew she wasn't recognized.

Once she was back in her car she steeled herself for the next step. She had decided that she needed an informed opinion about the painting and the only person she felt she could turn to at the moment was Armand.

She knew other artists and gallery owners who were knowledgeable about art, but she knew that Armand would be discreet and not inform the authorities. In fact he would relish being an accomplice.

Hannah drove down the sand road to the bay beach and Armand's cottage. She parked next to his jeep, took a deep breath, and walked around to the front of the house. She knocked several times before she heard someone stirring. Armand appeared at the screen door, hair tousled, chest bare, with a towel hastily wrapped around his waist.

Hannah's heart sunk but she assumed a business-like manner.

"Good morning Armand," she said. "I hope I didn't wake you." She looked pointedly at her watch which registered 10:15.

He shook himself awake and then grinned when he saw who was at his door. "Ah, Hannah! You've finally come to model for me."

"No I haven't," she replied firmly. Then added, "Go put some clothes on. I want to know if you can answer some questions about a painting."

She had used her best school teacher voice and tone which seemed to work since Armand immediately left and returned a few minutes later dressed in shorts and a t-shirt.

"Come in Hannah. Do you want a cup of coffee? I need one. I had a late night."

"Carousing?" she asked taunting him at bit.

"No," he replied and then said something vague about being out late on the water fishing with friends.

Hannah was suspicious and wondered what he really could have been doing late at night on the water. "Meeting a boat with a load of illegal drugs is the most likely reason," she thought. She quickly put this idea out of her mind since she had other things she wanted to discuss.

In a few minutes they were sitting on his porch, coffee in hand. Hannah unrolled the painting she had taken from Brocton's basement.

"How much do you know about stolen art?' Hannah asked Armand bluntly. He looked at her a bit puzzled and for once stopped being evasive and answered directly. "I am an artist and my work sells for sizeable sums of money. Perhaps you would be surprised to know that I actually trained as an artist."

Hannah quickly demurred, "No I wouldn't Armand. It is obvious that you have a great deal of talent and that you take your work seriously, even if you are a bit of a rogue."

"A rogue!" he laughed. Then he became serious again. "I spent four years at RISD and then three years at an art institute in Florence, Italy. During that time I sculpted and painted but also studied art theory, art history, learned about the great collectors of art over the ages and," he paused for effect, "researched the topic of stolen art, especially during World War II."

"Perfect!" said Hannah focusing his attention to the painting she had unrolled on the floor. "Do you know anything about this? And can you tell if it is authentic?"

He studied the woodland scene with the goddess Diana accompanied by a wolf hound, then reached into his pocket for his iPhone. "There are a number of websites where you can check stolen art."

He spent a few minutes doing various searches and then looked up and nodded. "Here it is. This painting was stolen by the Nazis from a Jewish family in Berlin at the start of the war. And I am pretty certain it is authentic. I can tell by the canvass and type of oils used. Where did you get it?"

Hannah told him the story of Lola wanting to search the basement of Brocton's gallery for the mirror and how they got locked in and the subsequent problems with the police.

Armand started to laugh but then stopped. "It would be funny except we are talking about Nazi loot. What was Brocton doing with it?"

"I don't know," Hannah answered. "But it's been stored away for some time. The painting was wrapped in old blankets that were covered with dust." She then decided to tell him everything. "What is even more intriguing is that Maddie had a photo of this painting and a few others in her house. I have reason to believe that all of them were stolen."

"Motive for a murder?" Armand asked.

Hannah was about to take her leave when Armand stopped her. "You have been honest with me. Now I want to tell you something."

Realizing that he was being serious for once, Hannah sat back down and gave him her full attention.

"The police were here after the murder asking if I had heard anything unusual the night of Maddie's death, especially from the water."

Hannah nodded encouragingly.

Armand continued, "I told them I didn't remember hearing anything unusual." He grinned and looked at her. "I told them I sleep deeply, like an innocent baby."

"Right," replied Hannah sarcastically.

"Actually, that night like last night I was out on the water," he hesitated and added, "fishing. So my motor was off and I could hear sounds across the bay."

"Did you hear something?"

"It was a dark night with no moon so I didn't see anything but I thought I heard the sound of a motor boat with the motor throttled down. I couldn't be absolutely sure where the sound came from. I looked over the water, but I didn't see any running lights. I thought it was a bit strange being on the water without lights but put it out of my mind."

"You probably ignored it because some nights you too are out on the water with a throttled down motor and no lights so you won't be detected," Hannah responded.

"That is my business," Armand said angrily. "I am just telling you what I heard." He then emphasized, "I didn't tell the police."

"Maybe you should," Hannah suggested lightly. "The police think that Maddie was nearly strangled and was unconscious when her body was thrown in the water. The murderer wanted it to look like suicide or an accident."

Armand stood up and stretched then looked down at Hannah with a grin. "Come over here," he motioned to her. "I will show you the choke hold."

She looked at him suspiciously. "What do you mean?"

Armand ran his finger alongside her neck. "Stop it!" she demanded moving away from him.

"Surely you aren't so naive that you don't know about the choke hold," he said laughing. "Couples use it to enhance the moment of orgasm. Pressure is put on the carotid artery which deprives the brain of blood and this adds to powerful sexual arousal."

"Of course I have heard of it," replied Hannah. "A number of years ago a member of the British Parliament trying for just such an arousal asphyxiated himself by accident."

"Yes it does have its dangers when one isn't an expert," Armand purred.

"Which you are, I take it," Hannah challenged.

The artist laughed and continued. "Actually it is very tricky. This type of pressure on the carotid artery is taught to military personnel to subdue an enemy and in personal safety classes for self-defense. You have to choke the victim just so long to make him unconscious. If it is done right the victim can be resuscitated, but if done too long the victim will die."

Hannah added, "And in the case of Maddie the murderer didn't bother to resuscitate her and instead threw her unconscious body in the water where she drowned."

"Or died from lack of oxygen to the brain," Armand said.

"But if you ever want to get the maximum sexual high," Armand said leaning toward her, "you know where to come. Pun intended."

"You are disgusting!" Hannah said as she moved to leave. "But I thank you for your help. I am going to show the painting to Chief Lee but I won't say anything about what you heard the night of the murder. You'll have to decide if you want to tell her. But be aware that the motor boat you heard might be tied to Maddie's death."

"If I tell the police I will be asked all kinds of questions which I'd rather not answer. I will wait to see what is happening with the investigation before I say anything."

Hannah returned home to find Martin putting the kayaks on the roof of the Volvo. They had an early lunch and headed for the town landing near the yacht club. As they paddled out of the mooring field Martin pointed to a 25 foot Grady White. "I am pretty certain that is the boat Troy Oliver is using this summer. He told me he had a mooring here. It is a very nice boat and rather expensive."

They kayaked nearly to Bellamy Spit when Hannah maneuvered her boat close to Martin's. "We've been out here over two hours. Maybe we should head in."

"Okay," he replied. "But it won't take us very long to return. The tide just turned and the wind picked up and it will be at our backs."

Martin was right. In just over an hour they were sitting on the beach next to their kayaks. Hannah thought this was the time to tell Martin about the stolen painting. She told him the whole story including Armand's confession that he had lied to the police about not hearing anything the night Maddie died. When she finished Martin started to scold her about going to Armand's alone but then stopped and said, "I think you should tell Chief Lee about this as soon as possible. Can I invite her for dinner? Jeff too?" he asked retrieving his cell phone from the dry bag in his kayak.

"What about Lola? Should we ask her? She is involved in this too."

Martin hesitated a moment and then said, "No I don't think so. If it is just us, Miyu might reveal more about the case. She would never talk about it in front of Lola. Plus it is Saturday. Lola will be at the theater."

Hannah showered quickly and then turned her mind to dinner. "Not much in the house," she said to Martin. "But there is basil from the farmers' market. I can make a pesto sauce, pasta and a green salad. What about dessert?"

"Put a little Kahlua on vanilla ice cream. That'll make a nice dessert," was his reply.

When they finished dinner, Miyu, Jeff, Martin, and Hannah sat in the small sunroom watching the sky turn a striking magenta, the last effect of a spectacular sunset. Conversation over dinner had been awkward since the charge against Hannah of breaking and entering was on everyone's mind but no one wanted to speak about it. This was, however, the time for Hannah to explain about the stolen painting she had found in Brocton's basement. She was hesitant, unsure as to how the Chief would react. Explaining that she had something important to say, she asked that neither Miyu nor Jeff ask any questions until she was finished with her account. She reminded them of the photos of paintings that Maddie had in her cottage and how Trudy had recognized them as photos of stolen art.

"You already know about all of this," Hannah said. Chief Lee nodded.

Hannah continued, telling the story of her adventure with Lola but now she included the fact that she had found a painting that matched one of Maddie's photos in Brocton's basement. She told about her visit to Armand and that he agreed that the painting was authentic and most likely stolen by the Nazis during World War II.

Chief Lee was amazed.

When she finally digested the information she said, "I appreciate that Armand is an artist and well versed in these things but before we jump to conclusions we will have an expert look at this. Lt. Connolly used one of the curators from the Museum of Fine Arts to identify Maddie's photos. I will ask him to bring the painting to Boston for identification."

She paused, "You do have the painting don't you?" she asked Hannah.

Hannah left the room and returned with the rolled canvas. Hannah's hands shook as she unrolled it, realizing the value of the work.

Chief Lee phoned Lt Connolly and Hannah sensed tension and excitement in their conversation.

When she finished her phone call the Chief seemed relaxed and actually started to laugh. "Wait until I tell Evan about how you hid the painting. Evan is the police officer who arrested you. He is a summer hire and has been quite cocky. When he learns that you managed to hide a painting under a blanket and then ditch it behind some bushes, it will take the wind out of his sails for a while."

The mood seemed right for Martin to ask about the charges against Hannah and Lola.

Chief Lee answered that Brocton was the key to the situation. "It all depends on whether he wants to press charges. With this new information who knows what will happen?"

She paused then said, "Since this involves you, I will tell you that we have not been able to locate Brocton. We have checked the major art shows and auctions in the Boston area but no one remembers seeing him. Of course that doesn't mean he wasn't there. However, we have not been able to contact him. He isn't answering his cell phone or his emails."

"Does this mean that the case against Gerard is now weaker?" asked Hannah.

"The stolen painting does add a new dimension, but the case against Gerard is still strong especially after we found traces of Maddie's DNA on his sailboat."

After Jeff and Miyu left Hannah said to Martin, "The DNA evidence really doesn't mean much. Maddie could have been out for a sail with Gerard anytime. I am sure they had things to talk about since they were still married and a sailboat would be a good place to talk and not be overheard."

"I agree," said Martin. "A good lawyer will have Gerard out of jail in a few days."

Chapter 22

Sunday dawned cool and overcast. Martin gathered baskets and clamming rakes and debated on whether to wear his waders. Hannah searched the basket of old clothes they kept in the basement for a wind breaker. When they got to the Mayo Bluff parking lot there were only a few cars.

"We are a little on the early side," said Martin.

"Either that or the cold weather is keeping people away," Hannah replied as she walked toward the water. There was a breeze from the south, which had created waves that were unusually high for the bay side.

"We are going to get very wet," she moaned as Martin walked ahead of her into the water.

Although Hannah was in water only up to her knees, the waves splashed around her and very quickly she was soaked. She thought about going back to the car to wait for Martin when she felt the unique scratch as she passed her rake over a clam. Hannah was now hooked. She kept working the same area and was rewarded with clam after clam. They were the small littlenecks that she liked to use in clam pasta. In forty-five minutes she had filled her pail and realized that she felt quite chilled. She retreated to the car, started the engine and put on the heat. A few minutes later Martin joined her. He was walking with Ben and when they reached the car Hannah opened the window to say hello.

"Ben was telling me that the Rhodes regatta has a 4 o'clock start this afternoon," Martin said to Hannah.

"I think we'll only do a couple of races," Ben explained. "With your boat out of commission and Gerard under arrest we'll probably only have three boats. Not much of a regatta, but I promised Doc I'd crew for him. It is going to be cold on the water. Do you or Hannah want to crew? I'll stay home, dry and warm."

They wished him good luck and started for home. On the way they passed Brocton's gallery.

"Look!" Hannah exclaimed. "Brocton's car is in the driveway. I am going to call Chief Lee," she said getting her cell phone from the glove compartment. "She may not know that Brocton is back."

Patrolman Santos answered the phone and told Hannah that Chief Lee was not at the station. Hannah was reluctant to tell him about Brocton. She was mulling over what to do when they arrived home.

They both took hot showers and put on dry clothes. Martin then phoned Jeff who told him that Miyu was with him at High Crest Beach at the annual life guard competition. "I am covering it for the paper and she was asked to be one of the judges. There are 12 teams this year. They competed in the run-relay, the swim relay, swim rescues, and ironman. It's cold and windy," he added. "The swimming events were really hard. Everything is just about finished so we should be able to leave in a half hour."

"Tell, Miyu, that Brocton is back. Your mother and I saw his car at the gallery. We'll drive to your house and meet you there," Martin replied.

"When you get there, do us a favor and start a fire in the wood stove. We are freezing!"

Brocton's car was still in the driveway when the Brewsters arrived at Jeff's. Within a few minutes Jeff's old truck rattled down his drive. "I am so cold," he said teeth chattering. "Thanks dad for making a fire," he added rubbing his arms and legs in front of the stove. "Miyu went directly to Brocton's gallery. Lt. Connolly is meeting her there. She was shivering when we left the beach but turned on the patrol car heater. I hope she has thawed."

Hannah was impatient. "Do you think we can go over to Brocton's?" she asked.

"If Miyu didn't invite you I don't think you should go. This is police business and you, dear mother, are not the police even though you do get yourself mixed up in things."

For Hannah the rest of the afternoon dragged on. Ben had phoned Martin asking him again, this time seriously, if he would crew that afternoon. The winds were strong and Doc wanted three people in his boat for more stability. While Martin was on the water, Hannah paced. She finally decided to drive to Mayo Beach to see how the regatta was progressing. Looking through binoculars she saw that there were four boats racing. Three of the boats she recognized as belonging to Ted, Doc, and the Nuns. There was a fourth boat that was unfamiliar. They were tacking and the wind was causing them to heel quite a bit but everyone seemed in control. She watched as the race ended unsure who had won. They all seemed very close to one other. She sat on the rocks at the breakwater scanning the bay for other boats. She spotted Troy in a Grady White heading out of Billingsgate Bay toward Eastham.

"Not the best day to be on the water," she thought. "But that is a well-built boat with a powerful motor so he won't have any problems, except for being cold that is."

When she looked back at the sailboats they were dispersing and heading for their various moorings.

Hannah stopped at the French bistro to buy a baguette and as she was leaving Dixie, Jeff's editor, waved and joined her. "Today is one of those cold days you sometimes get in the summer," she said, greeting Hannah. "All day the paper has been getting phone calls from tourists asking what the weather will be like tomorrow and what should they do instead of going to the beach. The receptionist is getting frustrated and wants to tell them that we are neither the Weather Channel nor the Tourist Bureau. I made it clear to her that tourism is a big part of the Cape's economy and we must be as helpful as possible. But, of course, I am not the one answering the incessant phone calls."

She then added, "Well at least it is a change from phone calls asking about Maddie's murder. We were getting a few dozen of those every day. The cold weather today and Gerard's arrest have made the murder a back page story."

"Speaking of stories, Hannah, you've been involved in a few escapades recently. You found Gerard in the Berkshires. You've been charged with breaking and entering at Brocton's gallery. We didn't write an article about the charge against you and Lola. I must be getting soft-hearted but Jeff asked me to put a hold on the story. It was, however, in the court report. Arrest and arraignments are always public knowledge."

Hannah mumbled a thank you.

"Actually there have been a number of stories lately that we haven't been able to print mainly because we can't corroborate them. Reporters are told all kinds of things, usually in confidence. Most of what we hear is based on local gossip and hearsay. For example, we were told that the police have their eye on Armand as a member of a drug ring. He's been seen in his boat more than once as it headed out of the bay at sunset. Now what is he doing going boating at night? Sounds suspicious to me, but we can't print anything because we have no proof. Then there is Brocton Phillips. Is it true he has disappeared? Lt. Connolly was asking a lot of questions about him lately."

Hannah remained silent.

Dixie continued, warming up to the subject, "Plus we've heard rumors that Maddie had a nice little estate in stocks and bonds which Gerard, as her husband, will inherit."

"Do you believe any of this?" Hannah asked.

"Who knows?" Dixie shrugged. "As I said we don't have any proof. But I've been a reporter for over thirty years and sometimes my best leads started as rumors."

Hannah's head was spinning as she drove home to prepare the clam pasta for dinner.

Chapter 23

"What a change in the weather," Hannah exclaimed the next morning as she stood on the deck in the sunshine. Martin agreed but cautioned, "The weather forecast warned that it could become unsettled again."

"Well right now it looks as if this could be a perfect summer day."

She readied herself to go to Orleans to help her friend, Juliet, set up an exhibit at Snow Library on diamondback terrapins.

"Let's kayak the ponds this afternoon. What time will you be back?" Martin asked.

"No later than two," she answered gathering her purse and keys. "By the way, Miyu left her sweater here the other night. I am dropping it off at the station before going to Orleans."

As she was leaving the phone rang and she heard Martin talking with Troy Oliver. He was reassuring him. "Don't worry, Troy," he said. "Hannah hasn't mentioned that your mother was a writer to anyone. As a matter of fact none of the people we talked to in Hoosac said anything about you getting your ideas from her. I think what Hannah meant was you probably inherited your talent from your mother."

Lt. Connolly was getting out of his state police vehicle as she parked by the station. As always he looked formidable in his uniform, hat, and dark glasses. "I heard the breaking and entering charges against you and Lola have been dropped," he said looking at her rather severely. They were immediately buzzed through security. Before Hannah could answer Chief Lee motioned Connolly to her office leaving Hannah standing in the hall. She thought about leaving the sweater at the security desk when she caught a glimpse of Brocton. Hannah was curious. Using the sweater as an excuse she entered the chief's office.

Brocton looked miserable. Instead of his usual dapper appearance he was rumpled and unshaven. "Hannah," he said with a groan, "I didn't sleep a wink all night. I lied about going to Boston for an art sale. Instead I went to stay with an old friend where no one could contact me. I needed to do some soul-searching."

Before the Chief or Lt. Connolly could ask her to leave, Brocton poured out his story. "This morning I decided to get everything out in the open."

He looked at the two officers. "I lied again yesterday when I told you I got that painting as part of a large lot. I told you I wanted two paintings in the lot but they came as part of a package. I had to buy everything."

"Okay, so now tell us the truth," commanded Connolly.

Brocton slumped even further in his chair. "I bought it from a disreputable dealer. I should have known better. I suspected it was stolen but I never checked. Later I was afraid so I rolled it up and hid it in my basement."

"Lydia's basement," Chief Lee said pointedly. "By analyzing the dirt on the blankets you used to hide the canvas, we know the painting was originally in Lydia's basement not yours."

"Why Lydia's?" asked Connolly.

Brocton hesitated, "You know that our two buildings were attached when they were on Billingsgate." He looked at Hannah when he said this. She nodded in confirmation.

"So," urged Connolly.

"For a long time the two buildings were attached here in Oyster Town until I decided to move mine across the street. Better for business. I don't remember why I put the painting in Lydia's side of the basement. There was a door connecting the two basements. Maybe I was having work done to my boiler or something, and I didn't want the painting there. I didn't want workmen to see it."

He then rushed on, "I forgot about it until Lola moved into the apartment above Lydia's antique shop. I was so afraid she would find it. I dreamed up schemes to get her to move. Then when she said she was going to clean the basement to give that scoundrel Armand storage space I really panicked. That's when I offered to help her. I found the painting and put it in my basement. I'm not sure what I would have done with it if you hadn't found it, Hannah."

"Thank goodness that is over. I feel so much better." Brocton mopped the sweat on his brow and tried to smooth the wrinkles in his shirt. "I must look like something the cat dragged in," he said with a wry smile. "Time to go home and make myself presentable."

Just as he reached the door Lt. Connolly called his name. He turned. "Just one more question," the Lieutenant said fixing his eyes on Brocton. "Do you know a man named Ed Schor?"

Brocton hesitated, as if searching his memory. "No I don't think so," he replied and started to leave again.

Connolly stepped in front of him and commanded, "Think about it! Isn't it true that he gave you the painting to hide for him?"

If Brocton looked bad earlier he looked terrible now. "Do I need a lawyer?" he nearly whispered.

"You decide," said the Lieutenant.

Brocton crumpled into a chair and asked, "How much do you know?"

"Enough to know that you lied to us yesterday and lied to us again this morning," said Chief Lee in a tone that made Hannah shiver. Brocton lowered his head and nodded dejectedly. "Yes, I lied. But how did you know?"

Chief Lee answered quietly, "Your neighbor, Lola."

Brocton looked at her puzzled.

The Chief continued, "When Jeff and his friends cleaned out Lydia's basement, finishing what you were supposed to do, they found a diary kept by Lydia and gave it to Lola. Of course she was curious and started reading it. She came across a passage describing the painting so she brought the diary to us."

"The diary puts you in the center of things," the Chief continued. "It described how Ed Schor asked you and Lydia to hide the painting. He stole it at the end of World War II. Lydia wrote that his unit was looking for Nazi loot as well as stashes of guns and armaments. He was one of the first GIs to check a salt mine in Austria where he found several pieces of art work that the Nazis had stolen and hidden to be retrieved after the war. Ed Schor took one of the smaller paintings and hid it in his knapsack. Years later he asked you both to hide it for him. For some reason you both agreed. Why?"

There was silence in the room.

"So you admit that you knew it was stolen," Connolly asked.

"Maybe I better call my lawyer," was Brocton's response.

Chief Lee and the Lieutenant exchanged glances and the Chief told Brocton that they were contacting a special organization that dealt with art stolen by the Nazis. "We might still be able to charge you with receiving stolen goods."

Then the Lieutenant added ominously, "We also might connect this to Maddie's murder so don't leave the area."

Brocton staggered out of the office but then turned defiantly. "In that case, I am going to press charges too. I will see Mrs. Brewster and that neighbor of mine, Lola, in court! They are guilty of breaking and entering."

It was Hannah's turn to slump into a chair. "Oh dear," she murmured. "I thought all that was over."

"That's what happens when you break the law," Lt. Connolly said sharply.

"In your case, Hannah, there are now extenuating circumstances," said Chief Lee trying to calm her. "Put it out of your mind for now."

"I wonder what else Brocton has lied to us about?" mused Connolly. "For example we know that he tried to sell the painting on the black market on at least three occasions."

At that moment the phone rang. The Chief spent a few minutes in conversation. When she hung up she said triumphantly, "We have an interesting connection. Ed Schor was Maddie's uncle."

Hannah and Connolly stared at her.

"Maddie must have known Brocton had the painting," Hannah finally said. "That was the reason she had a photo of it."

"There is more," said the Chief. "Brocton's father and Ed Schor were in the same division during the war. According to army records they were both in Austria as the war ended."

"You have been doing your research," said Hannah somewhat astonished by how much they had learned.

"So Brocton's father could have been helping an old war buddy, getting his son to hide the painting," surmised the state policeman. "Or he could have been in on the theft from the beginning. Or he could have asked his son to sell it."

"Whatever," answered Chief Lee, "with his father involved it has given us a reason why Brocton was willing to hide the painting or possibly fence it."

"But why would Lydia get involved?" asked Hannah.

"In the dairy Lydia indicates she felt some sympathy for Ed Schor. Who knows why? A slight romance?" the Chief said.

Hannah looked at her watch, realizing she was late. She had so many questions to ask but knew they had to wait since her friend, Juliet, would be wondering where she was. However, as she rose to go she said, "Maddie knew about Brocton and the stolen painting. Maybe he really does need a lawyer."

Chapter 24

Juliet was busy setting up her exhibit when Hannah arrived at the library apologizing for being late. "No problem," responded Juliet. "I appreciate your coming to Orleans to help me. I am so familiar with diamondbacked terrapins that I sometimes leave out basic information and give too many esoteric details. What I need is a layperson like yourself to look over my material."

They worked steadily. Hannah read over the various items to be put in the exhibit. In it Juliet had explained that diamondbacked terrapins were considered a threatened species in Massachusetts but the healthiest population in the Commonwealth was on Cape Cod.

"Your neighborhood is a perfect habitat for the terrapins," Juliet explained to Hannah. "They inhabit salt marshes, tidal flats, estuaries, and coves. All of these are major features in Bog Bay and Grampus Creek. They also need dry sandy upland spots nearby for their nests. There are about nine marked nests in your area at the moment. When the Audubon Society knows where eggs have been laid someone goes out and covers the nest with a wire cage to protect it from predators."

"We've been watching those nests," Hannah replied. "According to information in your exhibit the hatchlings will start to appear in late August and early September."

"I hope a lot of people look at this exhibit. I think the more people know about these turtles, the more they will be protected," Juliet said as she took a last critical look at the display.

They were about to leave when Hannah's cell phone rang. The call was from Troy. She answered and told him she was at Snow Library just finishing up a project and would return his call in a few minutes.

"That was Troy Oliver," she explained to Juliet. "Do you know him?"

"I do," Juliet replied. "I know him from my yoga and karate classes. Lots of the women find him charming, but I find him a bit egotistical. We are both professors and as a professional courtesy, I always inquire about his work but he rarely asks about mine."

They gathered their belongings and as she drove away, Juliet thanked her again.

After seeing Juliet off, Hannah returned Troy's phone call.

He explained he wanted to take the boat trip to Provincetown he had promised her and Martin. "I'd like to do it this afternoon. I know it is last minute. I spoke with Martin and he thought you both could make it. We can have a late afternoon drink and get back to Oyster Town before dark."

Hannah agreed to the trip.

"My boat is not at its usual mooring. Do you know the small boat landing off Bridge Road in Eastham?"

Hannah acknowledged that she did. Troy continued. Could she meet him there at about four? He rambled on telling her that his friend who owned the boat wanted to sell it.

"He is thinking of buying something smaller. Something he can keep in front of his house in Falmouth and store in his yard." Troy explained that he brought the boat to the landing in Eastham the day before so the potential buyer could see it. "The guy who is interested in buying the boat lives in one of the houses nearby. Then it got quite rough so I left the boat there and got a ride back to Oyster Town."

Hannah commented on the cold and windy weather of the previous day adding, "I thought I saw you on the water yesterday."

"So," said Troy. "Can you meet me in Eastham? Don't bother calling Martin to tell him where to meet. I'll do it since I have some questions to ask him about sailboats. I now think I should buy one since I probably won't have the use of the Grady White much longer."

He finished by saying, "The Eastham landing is probably a good place to meet anyway since it is a straight shot to Provincetown. It will be quicker and probably easier to get around Billingsgate. When we get back I'll leave the boat in Eastham. The buyer wants to try it out. He didn't yesterday due to the weather. I can get a ride back to Oyster Town with you or Martin."

Hannah agreed to meet him at the landing but was a bit miffed. It was certainly out of the way for Martin to drive to Eastham.

She decided she needed some warmer clothing for the trip. She phoned Martin to ask him to bring a sweater and windbreaker but there was no answer.

"No sense in leaving a message," she thought. "I have some time to kill and can use a new sweatshirt." She drove to a seasonal shop where she purchased a hoodie with a Cape Cod logo. Feeling more prepared for the trip she headed to Eastham.

Troy Oliver was waiting on the small beach when Hannah arrived. "Where's your car?" she asked after greeting him. Troy pointed to one of the homes overlooking the landing. "I left it in the driveway of the man who is thinking of buying my friend's boat," he replied as he helped Hannah into the motor boat.

The tide was coming in. Troy started to reset the anchor to remain close to shore so Martin could get in the boat when he arrived. Fifteen minutes passed and no Martin.

"Did you tell Martin the change in plans? Did you tell him we were meeting here rather than at my mooring in Oyster Town?" Troy finally asked Hannah.

Surprised, Hannah answered, "No. You told me you would call him. You said you wanted to talk about sailboats with him and would let him know the change in plans."

"Damn!" Troy swore. "I'm sorry. I've been so busy that I can't keep track of things. It's my fault. We'll have to go to Oyster Town to pick him up. No big deal. We have plenty of time to get to P-town. Plus it is a nice day to be on the water."

Hannah agreed but then worried a bit about the wispy clouds that were quickly developing. That could mean a weather change. She was thankful she had put on her sweatshirt.

Troy maneuvered the boat out of the small landing. He was very cautious.

"There are some sand bars in this area and I am not all that familiar with this boat," Troy said explaining why he was progressing so slowly. After a few moments they were in deeper water and heading northwest. This direction took them toward Billingsgate Bay where they would then turn north toward the channel leading to the Troy's mooring and Martin.

Suddenly, Troy cut the engine. Startled, Hannah asked if there was something wrong with the boat.

"No," Troy replied. "I want to talk for a minute and don't want to shout over the engine noise. I heard a rumor that Brocton was at the police station this morning and has hired a lawyer. Do the police think he is involved in Maddie's death? And what about Gerard? Hasn't he been charged with murder?"

Hannah was evasive knowing she should not reveal what she had learned that morning at the police station. "My gut feeling is that neither Brocton nor Gerard are murderers. There is some other factor in all of this."

She thought for a few minutes then continued, "Maddie talked about knowing secrets in the town. Both Brocton and Gerard had secrets but why did Maddie come back to town when she did? Brocton and Gerard have lived in Oyster Town for a long time. If she was going to reveal their secrets why didn't she return a few years ago? Something doesn't feel right to me. Maybe it is the timing."

Hannah continued to muse about Maddie when it hit her. "The timing!" she said to herself. "The timing in Troy's books isn't right."

Troy looked at her strangely. "Is something bothering you?" he asked tight-lipped.

Hannah tried to remain calm, her mind racing. The books were most likely written at an earlier time period. Settings in the books were wrong – a tube station that is now closed; Highgate cemetery where gates are now locked; terms for old English money. Troy was also evasive when she talked about London. He didn't really know London.

It struck her. Troy didn't write the books. They were probably written by his mother. No wonder he is so prolific. He had a supply of mysteries that he probably changed slightly and then sent to his publisher. But he wasn't careful enough and critics picked up on some of the errors. He spent time writing at the library but that was a sham. He was writing scathing critiques not mysteries.

Did Maddie know that Troy was passing off his mother's work as his own? She and Martin had learned in Hoosac that Maddie had babysat Troy. Maybe she saw his mother writing or saw the manuscripts?

She was horrified by the next thought. Juliet said Troy was in her karate class. He would know how to apply a choke hold. Did Troy kill Maddie?

Troy seemed to be reading her mind. "I knew you would be trouble right after you told me about the London critics and errors in my books. I tried to get rid of both of you by cutting wires on your sailboat, but somehow you got lucky and survived. Then you went to my home town where you snooped some more." His boyishly handsome face had turned very ugly and Hannah thought he might be insane.

He pinned her against the steering wheel.

"Don't!" Hannah pleaded. "You won't get away with this. Be logical. Martin is waiting for us at your mooring. If anything happens to me he will know you were involved."

"Martin doesn't know anything," Troy laughed with a wild look in his eyes. "I never invited him to go to Provincetown today. He isn't waiting. I lied. But he may come to the same conclusions that you have so I will have to get rid of him too. No one will connect me to your death, and I'll figure a way to have an alibi for Martin's. Then I am getting out of Oyster Town as soon as possible."

He grabbed Hannah's throat and started to apply pressure. They struggled. The wind had increased causing the boat to rock. They both lost balance. As Hannah escaped his grasp she fell and struck her head. It was a glancing blow. Somehow she kept her wits about her. Hoping Troy would think the combination of the choke hold and blow to her head rendered her unconscious, Hannah went limp, fell against the gunwales and tumbled into the water.

She dove as deeply as she could, kicked off her shoes and peeled off her sweatshirt. She stayed under until she thought her lungs would burst. As she surfaced Troy was circling. He didn't see her. She dove again. When she surfaced again Troy was scanning the water to her right. Taking a deep breath she went down again. She was thankful that running and yoga had given her the ability to hold her breath longer than many people, but she knew she could not continue this much longer. When she could not stay under another second, she surfaced praying that she would be lucky again.

This time she saw the boat moving away from her and heading in the direction of the mooring field.

"He must think that I am dead," she thought as she gave a sigh of relief. But seconds later she was aware that the weather had changed. The wind was strong and the waves were becoming large, starting to swamp her. She panicked, realizing she would not be able to swim to shore in these conditions.

"Even if Troy thought I was still alive he was sure I couldn't survive in this," she thought. Trying to calm herself, she let the waves wash over her, desperately trying to think of a plan that would save her.

Then it came to her. She remembered a Christmas card her nephew had sent to her a few years ago. It was a photo of him standing on a buoy in Nantucket Sound. He had gone out by boat, climbed onto it while a friend took the photo.

Hannah managed to get her head above the waves and spotted a red buoy. Because Troy was uncertain about handling the boat, he had stayed in the channel. With the help of the tide and the little strength she had left she managed to reach the buoy and haul herself out of the water.

Looking around she saw some boats heading into the harbor. She waved to get their attention but with the weather getting worse the boaters were focused on getting into port. She had one last hope. She was wearing a bright orange jersey. She hitched herself higher up the buoy, stripped off the jersey and waved it overhead.

Finally she gave up. She tied the jersey to the buoy. She felt desperate and started to shiver. Recalling an Outward Bound course she and Martin had taken many years ago she knew that when hypothermia struck it was important to keep the vital organs warm. She huddled herself into a ball and waited. She was afraid of becoming weak or falling asleep and slipping into the water. She knew if that happened she wouldn't have the energy to crawl back onto the buoy.

Chapter 25

Martin looked at his watch again. "Hannah said she would be back by two and it's after three. I wonder where she is?" He didn't dwell too much on it. He thought that when the weather turned bad Hannah decided they weren't going to kayak. "She probably went shopping," he thought. At 4:30 when he hadn't heard from her he started to be a little concerned. "Maybe she had car trouble," he thought. "But she has her cell phone. Certainly she would have called."

It was at that moment the phone rang. Martin pounced on it seeing the call came from the Oyster Town police department. It was Santos.

He greeted Martin and told him that his MG was parked at Boat Meadows. "You know, the small landing off Bridge Road in Eastham. A home owner in the area was returning from a shopping trip in Hyannis and saw some kids hanging around the car. He thought they might be up to some mischief so he called the Eastham police. They saw the Oyster Town beach sticker and called us. We ran the license number and found it was registered to you. Chief Lee said I should call and inform you."

Martin was now seriously worried. "Thanks Gino. Is Chief Lee there? I'd like to talk with her."

Martin explained to the police chief that Hannah had gone to Orleans to help a friend and was expected home a few hours ago. He also said that he was worried.

"Does Hannah know anyone who lives in that area? She could be visiting someone?"

"She meets new people from time to time but she hasn't mentioned knowing anyone at Boat Meadow. I don't know what to think," said Martin as he tried to stay calm. "I'd feel better if I talked with you in person. I am coming to the station."

Waves were crashing around Hannah and she found it increasingly difficult to hold on to the buoy. She knew being spotted was her only hope for rescue. She untied her orange jersey, hoisted herself higher on the buoy and tied it closer to the top. Exhausted and cold she fought off the panic that was starting to overcome her.

Then something caught her attention. Along with the roar of the wind and the slap of the waves Hannah heard a different sound. Listening she thought it could be a motor. She grabbed her jersey and waved it. She heard the sound again. This time she was certain it was a motor. Then she saw it. A boat was heading in her direction. She had been spotted. The captain approached the buoy on the leeward side. After a couple of attempts it was clear he felt he couldn't safely get close enough to her to pull her into the boat.

A voice that sounded familiar hollered above the din, "Catch the life preserver!"

Hannah indicated she understood. The first time the preserver was thrown it was blown away from her. On the second attempt it landed just a few feet away. She slid from the buoy into the water and swam as best she could toward it. She grabbed it and clung desperately as she was pulled to the boat and hoisted to safety.

She was shaking and disoriented. A coat was thrown over her as the familiar voice said, "Don't worry. You're safe."

She looked up to see Armand who grinned down at her. "Seeing you in just your bra makes me certain I want you as a model. A nude masterpiece."

Hannah at first felt exasperated by him. Then she started to laugh and then cry. As she shook uncontrollably Armand put a life jacket over the coat and sat her down. She then realized there was another person on board. Armand spoke to him in Spanish. She knew a bit of Spanish but didn't catch much of the conversation except that they seemed to be in disagreement. Then the other man shrugged his shoulders, giving into Armand's arguments. He started piloting the boat toward shore.

"If you don't mind, Hannah," said Armand, "we are making one stop before I get you to the marina."

Hannah didn't care how many stops they made. She was rescued.

It was very choppy but the boat cut through the waves and soon Hannah could see they were just off the beach in front of Armand's cottage. When they were in only a few feet of water the stranger jumped from the boat. Armand handed him a large cooler. The two men exchanged a few words, and then Armand turned the boat toward the marina.

"Everything is going to be okay. You are lucky I am an artist with an eye for color. It was the orange cloth that caught my attention," he said as he took his cellphone from his slicker pocket and called 911, explaining the situation and asking for an ambulance. He then radioed the Harbormaster.

Hannah smiled slightly but continued to shiver.

"You know the best way to deal with hypothermia?" Armand asked slyly.

Hannah knew what he was going to say. "I can't believe you, Armand. Don't you ever give up?"

"But it is true," he answered. "The best way to deal with hypothermia is two people of the opposite sex, naked, under a blanket. Shall we try?" He kept up a light banter but was getting concerned. Hannah was very pale and her lips and fingers had a bluish tinge. She also seemed disoriented and drowsy. He slowed the boat and moved her so she was sitting with him at the console. He reached over her to steer the boat, hoping that his body would add some heat to hers. Then he opened up the motor and sped as quickly as he could toward the harbor.

Everything was a bit of a blur to Hannah as they entered the harbor and pulled into the marina. She saw the harbormaster catching lines from Armand and securing the boat to the dock. As she was helped out of the boat by two EMTs she was aware of an ambulance with its lights pulsating. She was covered and strapped to a stretcher. As they started up the ramp, Martin ran forward and hugged her. He had been at the police station when the call from Armand came in. Jeff hovered nearby looking very worried as she was assisted into the ambulance.

A female EMT quickly helped her remove the few items of wet clothing she was wearing – pants, panties and bra and covered her in layers of blankets. An assessment was rapidly being made of her condition. By this time Martin had squeezed into the ambulance and was anxiously watching the procedures.

"Your body temperature has fallen to 94 degrees which is considered mild hypothermia," the male EMT told Hannah. She continued to shiver as she held her arm out from under the blankets while her blood pressure was taken.

A cup of hot water was held to Hannah's lips. "Sip it." As she drank and felt the liquid warm her mouth and throat she heard a siren. Shortly after, a second one. Hannah assumed that these were police cars which meant Chief Lee and probably Lt. Connolly had arrived. She was still shivering and found it difficult to talk but she was anxious to tell them about Troy.

"The EMT stopped her from speaking and said, "Let us finish our assessment of your condition and then you can talk."

Hannah tried to relax under the blankets and stay calm but they seemed to take forever. Finally one of the EMTs said to Martin, "We can take Mrs. Brewster to Cape Cod Hospital if you want, but we think she will be fine. The color is returning to her face. Her fingers and ears are no longer blue and her temperature has risen to nearly 95 degrees. She was lucky. According to Mr. DeCristo she was probably in the water for some time. When you get home you can get in bed together under a lot of covers. Your body heat will help her warm up."

Hannah laughed. "That is what Armand proposed to do with me on the boat." Then she added, "Take me home. I don't want to go to the hospital. I will be fine. All I need is to warm up and get some sleep."

Martin was unsure what to do when the EMT repeated that she was certain Hannah would be fine. "We will drive her home in the ambulance. Do a final check of her condition. After a release form is signed she can recuperate comfortably in her own home."

"Martin," Hannah called as he was exiting the ambulance. "I have to talk with Chief Lee. Ask her to come to the house."

She then blurted to Martin, "Troy Oliver is the one who cut our shrouds. He wanted to kill us. He murdered Maddie and just tried to murder me. He said he would murder you too."

Chapter 26

It was very blustery as Troy pulled up to his mooring. The beach was empty and he was certain no one had seen him as he tied up the boat and rowed to shore. He congratulated himself on the preplanning he had done. He lied to Hannah about parking his car at one of the houses at Boat Meadows. He had never intended to go back to Eastham with her. Instead he had tucked his car down a dirt path. He crossed the beach parking lot, walked a short way down the road and turned into the path. The entrance was nearly hidden by overgrown bushes. "If I had left my car in the parking lot at the beach, someone would have recognized it," he mused, feeling very smug as he drove toward Main Street.

"Now to establish an alibi," he thought cunningly. He drove to the library, took his laptop from the trunk and entered by the back door. From the small hallway he could see the circulation desk and the librarians. When both librarians were busy he quickly entered and slipped into one of the book aisles. Shortly afterward he approached the desk.

"Good afternoon," Mr. Oliver. One of the women greeted him. "Writing again today?"

Oliver smiled. "Yes, I have. And it has been a very productive few hours." He gave her his winning smile. "Your library seems to stimulate me. I do some of my best writing here."

Troy drove home and poured a scotch and soda, congratulating himself on successfully eliminating Hannah. It had been 'a very productive few hours'. He sipped his drink sitting by a window which overlooked Commercial Street contemplating how to get rid of Martin. A plan was just starting to formulate when he was shaken out of his reverie by the sound of sirens. Looking out the window he saw an ambulance racing in the direction of the marina. A few minutes later he heard two more sirens; one from an Oyster Town police car; the other from a state police car. Fear gripped him. "She couldn't have survived," he reasoned with himself. "They must have found her body. But how could her body have been found so quickly? Damn! Maybe someone rescued her."

Thinking frantically he quickly sketched out a plan. He kept a sizeable amount of cash on hand ever since Maddie's murder. "You never know what might happen," he told himself as he had stockpiled the money. He went to his small safe telling himself, "Well now I am going to need the cash."

He packed some clothes, got his computer and jumped in his car. He went to the drive-through window at the bank in Eastham and withdrew even more money. His plan was to drive to Hyannis, abandon his car at Cape Cod Community College and walk across the road to the bus stop at the Burger King. He'd take the bus to South Station and catch the train to New York City. "I will have to lie low in a hotel for a few weeks," he told himself. "But cities are pretty anonymous. I can easily get a studio apartment. I'll have to work somewhere for a while but eventually I can publish some books under a pseudonym. I still have a number of my mother's manuscripts. Plenty of people have 'gone to ground'. Look how long Whitey Bulger hid out. Years!"

Hannah crawled into bed and Martin and Jeff gathered blankets including a down comforter to help warm her. Chief Lee and Lieutenant Connolly stood over the bed as Hannah poured out her story. She described Troy's phone call to her in Orleans, meeting him in Eastham, and the attack on the boat.

Martin hugged her as she described the harrowing time spent on the buoy.

"You were very lucky Armand was on the water and spotted you," Chief Lee said. Then she mused, "I wonder what he was doing on the water with the weather getting so bad?"

Hannah was about to tell her about the other man on the boat and the cooler they unloaded near Armand's beach house, but stopped herself. Despite rumors about Armand being involved in drug operations, she had no proof that anything illegal was in the cooler. She knew she was rationalizing the situation but felt she should be loyal to Armand. After all, he had just saved her life.

Hannah started to shiver again but this time it wasn't so much from the cold but from the realization of the danger she had been in. Yes, her life had been at risk.

"What are you going to do about Troy Oliver?' she finally asked.

"He has vacated his house on Commercial Street. We think he left when he heard sirens going toward the marina. That probably panicked him. We have put out an APB with a description of Oliver and his car. It is unlikely he will get off the Cape," the Lieutenant answered.

"And we are posting someone here at the house for your security, just in case."

Hannah wanted to ask more questions but was too exhausted. Instead she looked at the group assembled by the bed and said, "I thought Martin was going to get his naked body in bed with mine. I was looking forward to that."

Chief Lee grinned and nodded to the others, "I guess we are dismissed."

Chapter 27

The next evening the Brewsters gathered on their deck overlooking the marsh and Bog Bay. Hannah lazed in the late day sun while Martin organized the bar, and Jeff played guitar. Lieutenant Connolly and Chief Lee arrived together. He was in uniform, but she was in shorts and a tee shirt. Armand in his ragged jeans was just behind them.

"Troy Oliver was apprehended yesterday as he tried to leave the Cape," Martin told Armand, after thanking him again for rescuing Hannah.

"That was quick work," was Armand's reply.

For Armand's benefit they explained what had happened. "His car was identified as he drove west on Route 6. We had lots of state and local police on the lookout for him," Lt. Connolly explained.

"The order to stop him was just being made when he left the highway at exit 6. The police decided to follow him until they could find a safe spot to pull him over. He was considered dangerous so we didn't want to apprehend him in a populated area."

Chief Lee continued the story. "When he took exit 6 he drove immediately to Cape Cod Community College. He parked at the far end of one of the parking lots. After that it was easy. He was arrested as he got out of his car."

"What did he say about Maddie and Hannah," Armand asked anxious to know if the police were facing a long drawn out investigation. He was anxious because he knew an extensive investigation would include him and he didn't like anyone prying into his activities.

"Once he knew Hannah was alive and well, he admitted to attacking her," Connolly answered. "He said he lost his temper. He refused to say why and refused to answer any questions about Maddie. Instead he demanded to have a lawyer."

"Martin and I learned all this yesterday," Hannah said. Then she directed her comments to Armand, "Before the police left us snuggling in bed."

"So what is the news since yesterday?" asked Jeff. "And can I put any of this in the paper?"

"Nothing you can write as yet," answered Connolly. "But we are certain we can make a good case against Oliver. We have the motive. He has a big ego and had to protect his reputation as a writer and a professor. He didn't want anyone to learn he was not the author of the books."

Chief Lee continued, "In his luggage the police found several manuscripts that we are sure were written by his mother and we can show how he changed some to create his books."

"And," she nodded to Hannah and Martin, "we will tie this to Maddie. Thanks to you, we learned she knew Troy as a child and she babysat for him so had access to his house. Maddie may have seen the manuscripts or his mother may have told her about them."

"And the attack on Hannah, using a choke hold, is pretty damning evidence," Connolly concluded. "We are pretty certain his lawyer will tell him to cooperate."

"You did a wonderful job," Hannah said thanking him. "I am so relieved."

Connolly turned to Miyu and said, "Couldn't have done it without Chief Lee. Second time I've worked with her. I think we make a great team. I still wish I could convince her to apply for a job with the state police and come to Boston."

Miyu smiled and joined Jeff in the hammock. Lieutenant Connolly looked puzzled for a moment and then grinned. "Now I get it. I have competition."

"A big strong, handsome man like you shouldn't have competition," a voice called out.

It was Lola, who had just arrived. She sidled up to the officer, stood on tiptoe, and snatched his cap putting it on her own head. "Relax. You're off duty."

He was about to protest, then laughed, picked up his back pack, went into the house to change into jeans and a casual shirt. Returning he sank into a chair and accepted a beer from Martin saying to him, "My work here is done for today. I might as well relax and enjoy the view," he said looking towards Lola who was slipping off her tee shirt to reveal a tiny polka dot bikini.

"My neighbor, and now good friend, Brocton Phillips, has been in a better mood lately," she told the group as she spread suntan lotion on her arms, giving the tube to Connolly indicating she wanted him to put some on her back.

"He said that some organization that keeps files on art stolen by the Nazis has a record of the family that owns the painting he hid. He was informed that they are not pressing charges. After all they are getting the painting back and he didn't steal it, only hid it."

Armand piped in, "I don't like Brocton, but I'm glad this is settled. It's time for things to return to normal in Oyster Town."

Everyone nodded in agreement.

Then Miyu said, "What is normal around here?" She looked hard at Armand. "For example what were you doing out on the water yesterday with the weather so bad? Whatever it was Hannah was lucky you were out there."

Armand glanced at Hannah. Her steady gaze let him know she had said nothing about the other man in his boat nor the stop they made at his house. He roused himself from a deck chair and went to his jeep. From it he took a large cooler, which Hannah thought she recognized.

"This, Miyu, is the reason I was out on the water." They all looked into the cooler and saw it contained several live lobsters. "I have several pots out in Cape Cod Bay. This is my contribution to tonight's meal."

Miyu looked at him, skeptically.

"I'll take you out to the pots someday to show you," he murmured to the police chief. "Just you and me – real cozy."

Jeff and Lola went for a swim. Miyu stretched out on the hammock with a glass of wine and Martin and Lt. Connolly went to get some pots to boil the lobsters.

Armand moved closer to Hannah and handed her a card. It was an ID. He gave her a sly grin and whispered. "Actually, I was on the water yesterday doing an off shore drug patrol for the FBI. Just call me Special Agent DeCristo.

Alice Iacuessa

Alice Iacuessa spent 30 years as an international school teacher. She lived in Germany, Venezuela, Luxembourg, and, for twenty-one years, in London, England. During all of that time she had a summer home on the Outer Cape. She and her husband split their time between Wellfleet and London. *Body in Bog Bay* is her second Oyster Town mystery.

Made in the USA
Charleston, SC
27 August 2013